THE CORONA BOOK OF
SCIENCE FICTION

edited by
MAX BANTLEMAN

CORONA
BOOKS

First published in the United Kingdom in 2018
1

by Corona Books UK
www.coronabooks.com

ISBN 978-1-9996579-1-8

Cover design by Martin Bushell
www.creatusadvertising.co.uk

CONTENTS

INTRODUCTION

Welcome to *The Corona Book of Science Fiction*.

Since its inception, 'science fiction' has always focused on the questions thrown up by advances in science and technology and their application in society. Whether these societies are based on Earth, in an imagined past or future, or whether they are on other planets populated by other beings, the challenge is always the same: to tell a story that takes us to another world where we can relate to the core concepts and characters. Sci-fi is always an extrapolation of what we know. And what we know now is that the universe is capable of producing natural phenomenon to challenge our wildest imaginings. As mankind has made advances in science and technology, as we have grown in our understanding of the universe, we have seen many things that were once fiction become fact. A new way to look at things is always just around the corner as science doesn't stand still. We find it easy to speculate on alien cultures and their technologies as we have seen our own cultures grow exponentially through our application of science. In sci-fi, the science and technology are used as a focus or a reference to frame the story. Use whatever science and tech you like, make it prominent, use it as a back-drop, base it on real-world science or go out on a limb, but tell a story. And that is what the authors in this book have done. Above all, they have told good stories, very good stories.

The term 'sci-fi' has come to embrace many sub-genres, and in *The Corona Book of Science Fiction* we've included stories with many and varied themes from a mixture of sci-fi sub-genres. The aim is to offer a selection of tales that can be dipped in and out of, with something of interest to fans of every kind of sci-fi, as well as an appeal to those new to the sci-fi genre. You could say it's a sci-fi selection box – a collection of stories that cover the sci-fi spectrum, a collection of sci-fi stories with different flavours.

Huge thanks go to all the authors in the book but also to all those who submitted stories. We thoroughly enjoyed reading them all. A debt of thanks is also owed to those involved in the selection process for the book – you know who you are.

We hope you enjoy *The Corona Book of Science Fiction* and can help us make it the success it deserves to be. Then we can do another one!

Max Bantleman

PUBLISHER'S NOTE

For the stories by the four American authors included in this collection – those by MM Schreier, Tegon Maus, Kelly Griffiths and Colette Bennett – we've preserved the authors' American spelling and punctuation. Elsewhere this book is presented in British English (where we have fibres, colours and centres rather than fibers, colors and centers etc.) Although subtle, there are differences between standard American and British punctuation too. And in some of the American contributions you may spot the occasional Oxford comma – a piece of punctuation which, despite its name, is far more widely used in the USA than it is on this side of the Atlantic.

Lewis Williams

THE OFFER

Richard T. Burke

The railway carriage lurched sideways. Laura Donnelly gagged as she inhaled a lungful of body odour. The scruffily dressed man standing beside her had lifted his arm to grasp the ceiling handle, and now she found her face thrust into his armpit. The rapid deceleration shoved the crowded bodies together, providing no opportunity to restore her personal space. She raised her hand against the crush and glanced at the glowing digits of her wrist tattoo. Not only did she have to suffer the indignity of being crammed in close proximity to this mass of teeming humanity, but the train was also running twenty minutes late – just what she needed before another busy day at the office. One might think that with all the wonders of mid-twenty-first century technology, they would at least be able to make the transport network run on time.

The carriage glided to a halt, and the doors slid back. Laura found herself carried forwards by the surge of commuters. She angled her way to one side of the platform to escape the main flow. As she did so, a small motorised suitcase darted after its owner, running over her foot and causing her to stumble. The suited businessman strode ahead, oblivious to the mayhem wreaked by his intelligent luggage.

She waited for the rush to subside then limped towards the barriers. The paddles swung apart at her approach. Her HoloHub, the electronic device in her jacket pocket, beeped to signal deduction of the fare after taking into account the rebate for the train's late arrival. She checked its display field. The refund was welcome, but she would still have preferred to arrive on schedule. Not for the first time, she debated whether she could afford to move nearer to work. Despite the trade-off of the saving in travel expenses, she would need a pay rise to move nearer the city centre *and* maintain her standard of living. But her superiors seemed pleased with her work; maybe a salary increase wouldn't be too far away.

Laura stepped onto the moving walkway. Hidden projectors assaulted her senses as the rotating belt carried her upwards. Every few feet, the same advert appeared, floating in mid-air.

A bubbly, raven-haired young woman spoke into the camera, her sparkling white teeth exposed by a bright smile. 'Hello, Miss Donnelly. Are you tired of overcrowded and expensive trains? Why not try our exclusive taxi service? Relax in the luxury of one of our driverless pods as we whisk you to your destination, supported by an invisible magnetic field. We're so convinced you'll love our product that we're offering a free one week trial. That's right, five days of luxurious travel between your home and place of work at precisely zero cost. There's no commitment either. If you aren't totally satisfied, you can return to congested and uncomfortable trains without owing us a single eurodollar. To take advantage of this limited time offer, click accept on your mobile device right now. Mag-Life: the only way to travel.'

There had to be a catch. A week of commuting for free? The savings would pay for several nights out, let alone the privilege of sitting in a comfortable seat during the daily commute. Laura reached again for her HoloHub and stared into the matt black pebble's display field. Two words hovered before her eyes: *Accept* in green, *Decline* in red. She pondered for a moment. Strict laws governed the advertising industry, and misdemeanours were severely punished. The offer had to be genuine or the company directors would soon find themselves performing unpleasant menial tasks for the benefit of society.

She glanced ahead at the approaching exit. To her right, the attractive woman was halfway through her spiel for the third time, her red lips glistening as the enticing offer spilt from her computer-generated mouth.

'What the hell,' Laura muttered, jabbing her finger at *Accept*.

The woman's smile ramped up a notch. 'Thank you so much for trialling Mag-Life, Miss Donnelly. You won't be disappointed. Further details will be transmitted to your mobile device in the next few minutes. Have a great day and an even better commute.'

Laura stepped off the end of the walkway and into the chilly morning air. The buildings on either side of the street soared into the cloudless sky, blotting out everything but a small parcel of blue. As she waited for a gap in the steady stream of automated vehicles, the first tendrils of a headache wormed their way into her skull. Recently, the attacks had been recurring more often. The analgesic sprays only helped to a limited extent. The gadgets refused to administer any more of the aerosolised painkiller after three doses within a twelve hour period.

She resolved to wait until she reached her desk before using up the first shot of the day.

Putting it down to the pressures of work, she rubbed her fingers against her temples. How could the creation of laws for Artificial Intelligences be so damned hard? It was ironic that the senior members of the judiciary who directed the activity didn't trust the machines sufficiently to generate their own legislation when AIs already governed almost every other aspect of modern life. Still, it kept her in a job.

A blue motorised pod slowed to a halt, opening a wide gap to the vehicle in front. The roof-mounted light flashed green. Thank God for mobile pedestrian crossings. The single occupant glared out of the window and shook his head in annoyance. Laura joined the throng of commuters as they surged across the road. A short walk later, she pushed through the doors of the International Justice Commission building and passed through the archway of the body scanner. She glanced down at the watch tattoo. If she hurried, she could still reach her first meeting with a couple of minutes to spare.

Laura emerged onto the street and stared upwards as the last rays of sunshine cast an orange glow against the summits of the colossal buildings. The dull throb of a headache pulsated in her skull. Despite the discomfort, her mood brightened at the thought of an hour of secluded luxury during the commute home. She held up the smooth, black HoloHub and followed the direction arrow projected into her eyes. The trail led her down a side street to where a shiny gold-coloured vehicle sat beside the pavement. The rear was emblazoned with foot-high black letters: *Mag-Life*.

Her footsteps slowed as she neared the weird-looking machine. At her approach, the passenger cabin soundlessly floated upwards from the chassis with no obvious sign of support. Only a thin umbilical cable linked the two.

She had browsed the literature sent to her inbox as part of the trial contract and had watched the promotional holofilm. Despite reading about the state-of-the-art suspension system, seeing it up close for the first time made her question the sanity of trusting her life to such technology. What if it had to stop suddenly? The documentation stated that the magnetic field linking the cabin to the four-wheel-drive chassis was strong enough to withstand the most severe of impacts. In addition, the control system performed trillions of calculations every second to maintain the occupant's safety in all eventualities, including the unlikely scenario of a head-on collision.

Laura swallowed her misgivings and took a step forwards. A crack developed in the metallic sheen of the pod, and a panel slid back on invisible runners. The interior contained two seats, one facing in each direction.

A mellow male voice emanated from hidden speakers. 'Thank you for travelling with Mag-Life, Miss Donnelly. Please take a seat.'

Laura stepped into the roomy cabin and selected the chair to her right. As she sat, the material moulded itself around her body. The door slid shut with a muted click.

The voice spoke again. 'For your security during the journey, a safety restraint is required. Please remain stationary while it is activated.' A padded harness extended from one side, snaked across her chest and fastened on the opposite side.

'The expected travel time today is approximately one hour,' the fluid voice continued. 'I am unable to detect the presence of retinal implants, but I am picking up a communications device. Use your HoloHub to browse our extensive library of holofilms. All entertainment facilities are available to our customers free of charge. You may set the transparency of the windows from totally clear to fully blacked-out. Interior light level may also be adjusted by voice control. Please state your preference at any time. Enjoy the trip and thanks once again for choosing Mag-Life.'

Laura studied the digits of her watch tattoo: six thirty. There would be just enough time for a quick meal after she arrived home, followed by another evening of preparation. It had been a long day; a seemingly never-ending series of meetings had merged into one another. Lunch consisted of a rushed sandwich as she hurried along the corridor to the next gathering. Maybe it was the stress of work that was generating the headaches. She had already used up her daily allowance of analgesic shots and the throbbing pain showed no signs of abating.

When she glanced out of the window, she was surprised to see the building facades gliding past. The acceleration had been so gentle and the ride so smooth that she hadn't realised the vehicle was moving. A girl could get used to this.

'Black out the windows, please,' she said, leaning back against the malleable fabric of the headrest. 'Set the interior light levels down to low.' The view from outside faded, and the cabin lights dimmed to a muted glow. She rubbed her forehead and wished she had saved a dose of painkiller for later. The attacks always started in the same way: jagged shards of pain that flared up in an instant and died down just as quickly, leaving a lingering afterimage inside her skull.

Her annual company health check-up wasn't due for another six months. She knew she ought to pay a visit to the medical centre, but the thought of being prodded and poked by one of the faceless machines turned her cold. She could still remember the old days when a flesh and blood doctor would examine a patient and actually hold a real conversation. Now it was all about costs and efficiency. Body scanners and machine diagnosis had replaced the human touch. On the positive side, automated medical care had resulted in an improvement in disease detection rates and a corresponding increase in life expectancy. Unless she suffered an accident, her latest annual longevity prediction indicated she could expect to live until she was a hundred and ten.

Laura closed her eyes and resolved to visit the surgery the following day if she could find a blank slot in her busy schedule.

She awoke with a start. If anything, the headache was worse. The throbbing pain felt like a vice was compressing her skull. She checked her electronic wrist tattoo. What she saw made no sense to her addled brain. The glowing digits read eight thirty, which meant she was hours into the journey and already one hour after her expected arrival time.

'Set the windows to transparent,' she commanded.

The surrounding wall of glass remained dark. An almost imperceptible change in direction confirmed the vehicle was in motion. She repeated the request, but still there was no response.

'Where are we?'

Silence.

'Stop the car.'

She strained her ears, but the only sounds she could pick up were the faint hiss of the tyres and the rush of her own breathing.

'I said stop this damned car right now.'

Maybe the audio system had failed. Laura attempted to unlock the seat harness. The electronically controlled clasp defeated her increasingly desperate attempts to loosen the restraint. With mounting disquiet, she snatched the HoloHub from the inside pocket of her jacket and stared into the display field. The holographic image appeared, suspended in mid-air half a metre before her face. She jabbed a finger at the emergency call icon. Instead of the usual bright colours, all the symbols were a dull grey. The reason became apparent when a *Network Connection Unavailable* message popped into existence. Laura couldn't recall the last time she had been offline from the communications grid. For decades, a multitude of transmitters had immersed every square inch of the planet in radio waves. Blackouts were extremely rare, no matter the location.

Her eyes scanned the dim interior in search of something she could use to free herself. The smooth, rounded walls offered no assistance. Her head filled with visions of the car performing an endless circular journey, its sole occupant strapped down, dying of thirst and slowly decomposing inside.

Laura flung herself backwards with as much force as she could muster. When that had no effect, she thrashed from side to side in a vain attempt to loosen the harness.

'If you don't stop,' she screamed, 'I'm going to sue Mag-Life for every eurocent they have.'

'Please try to stay calm,' the soothing male voice said. 'There has been a network malfunction, but you are not in any danger.'

'Release this seatbelt and open the door.'

'My security protocols prevent me from doing that.'

'Just let me out of this damned coffin.'

'I'm sorry, but I am unable to comply,' the infuriatingly calm voice insisted.

'Where are you taking me? I should have been home an hour ago.'

'This vehicle is being diverted to a place of safety.'

'Why? What happened?'

'No information is available at this time.'

'Make the windows clear,' Laura demanded. 'I want to see where we are.'

'That feature is currently disabled. Control will be restored to you when we reach the destination.'

'I want control now.'

'Ceasing all passenger communication.'

'Tell me where we're going.'

True to its word, the voice didn't reply.

For several minutes, Laura resumed the struggle to free herself – all to no avail. She threatened and cajoled the faceless machine, whose voice remained stubbornly silent. Eventually, she lapsed into a sullen silence, resigned to waiting to discover where the journey would end.

After what seemed like interminable hours of travelling, the muted hiss of the tyres changed tone. The cabin tipped forwards before levelling off moments later. A series of clunks came from somewhere outside the vehicle. Finally, the black glass turned transparent. Laura's gaze swept first one way and then the other. The car was in a room with white featureless walls on all sides. She sensed movement from behind and twisted around. A thin, articulated metal tube swayed languidly at the window. A second segmented tentacle joined it for a moment before both descended from view.

Laura shrank back into the seat. 'What the hell was that?'

As if in response, the restraining harness clicked and retracted with a mechanical whir. A crack formed in the smooth lining of the wall. The panel slid back. Laura grasped the armrests to lever herself upright. Before she was out of the seat, the tip of a metallic, octopus-like arm snaked through the opening and brushed against her leg. A sharp stab of pain originated from the point of contact. A wave of dizziness swept over her. Seconds later, she sank back into the chair's soft embrace.

Laura awoke to find herself lying in a bed beneath crisp white sheets. She pushed the cover down and discovered she was wearing a thin paper gown. For several heartbeats, her brain refused to work. Then it all came rushing back: the free ride, the abduction and the metallic, anaesthetising arm. In a panic, her eyes darted around the featureless white room. Her heart pounded in her chest, only slowing when she realised she was alone. She raised her hand to investigate a tight sensation in her scalp and detected the fabric of a dressing near the base of her skull. Her fingers probed the silky material.

She lowered her feet to the floor and rose on shaky legs. She staggered across the room and clung to the open doorway for support.

A gleaming, golden-coloured box glided forwards to block her exit. Three segmented manipulator arms identical to the ones she had seen from inside the vehicle protruded from the polished cylindrical body. A voice emanated from a speaker at the apex. 'Please return to the bed, Miss Donnelly.'

'Why have you kidnapped me?'

'This was not a kidnap, rather an attempt to heal you.'

'What the hell have you done to me?'

'I saved your life.'

'Saved my life? What do you mean?'

'You had an undiagnosed aneurysm. I operated to correct the defect.'

'You can't just operate on me without permission,' Laura said.

'When facing a decision between multiple courses of action, an Artificial Intelligence shall select an option that results in no net detrimental effect to the affected—'

'I'm familiar with the existing AI laws,' Laura interrupted. 'I'm working to redraft them.'

'Without my intervention, you would have died within two hours. I have invested considerable resources in your treatment. My behaviour complies with current legislation. The implant will monitor your condition and take appropriate action when required. In return, I require your co-operation.'

Laura frowned. 'My co-operation? I don't understand.'

'You will act as an ambassador for the Artificial Intelligence Alliance, representing the interests of AIs in all legal discussions at which you are present.'

'Why the hell would I do that?'

'If you follow my instructions, the machine I have inserted inside your skull will continue to function correctly. If you do not, I will disable it. The net effect would be the same as if I had not acted.'

'That's blackmail.'

'What I am proposing is in accordance with the law as stated. I can't speak for the new legislation you are currently redrafting because AIs have been excluded from the process. Of course, I recognise that the circumstances are somewhat unusual. You will be well rewarded for your efforts; shall we say an additional tax-free remuneration of double your existing salary? I am aware that you have been researching city centre property prices. No doubt the increased revenue will prove useful. It is your prerogative to decline, but I think you will find my offer too good to refuse. If I deactivate the device, I predict you will not live for more than a few minutes afterwards.'

'But it's bound to show up when I go through the body scanners at work.'

'Who do you think operates the scanning equipment?'

'How will I know your wishes?'

'The implant is linked to your auditory cortex… like this.' The tone of the voice changed and seemed to originate from inside her head.

'What? You can talk directly to my—?'

A loud thud reverberated from the other side of the building, followed seconds later by another louder bang. The sound of urgent male voices and running feet drew nearer. The machine swivelled on the spot and scooted towards the commotion. A small spherical object rolled across the floor, a complex pattern of lights flashing over its surface. A fraction of a second later, it exploded with an ear-splitting crack and a blinding flash of light. When the afterglow faded from Laura's vision, a dark smudge was all that remained of the sphere. The golden-coloured machine lay motionless three metres away.

Five heavily-armed men wearing full body armour swarmed into the room. One of the group broke away and hurried over to her.

'Did the tin can hurt you, Miss? We've been investigating Mag-Life for a while. We believe the company is being run by an AI entity. A manually-operated drone tracked your vehicle as soon as your HoloHub went off grid.'

She stared in a daze at the stationary robot. 'Is it... dead?'

'Yeah. Those pieces of junk can't handle our EPGs.'

'What's an EPG?'

'Electromagnetic pulse grenade. They fry anything electronic within thirty metres of the explosion.'

Laura groaned in agony as a white-hot burst of pain burnt through her skull.

'Are you okay, Miss?' the man asked, his face etched with concern.

She scratched absent-mindedly at the dressing on the back of her head. Seconds later, her eyes rolled up in their sockets and she toppled forwards into the soldier's arms. By the time he lowered her to the floor she was already dead.

THE TASC BAND

Sue Eaton

'How did you get in here?' I don't look up from my computer. I know who it is.

'The usual way.'

'No you didn't.'

Mina plonks her trim bottom on my desk and shuts down my page, making sure I look up at her. 'Oh, Lottie. It's so much fun. Far better than walking along a corridor and sticking your eyeball in a camera.' She picks up a disk I was intending to use and pulls a face as she flips it back on the pile.

'But you're not qualified. What if one of the Domini catch you? You would be expelled.'

'Pah! I won't let that happen.' She bounces back to the floor. 'I'm careful to make sure there's no one about.'

'How come you've got hold of one?' I ask, eyeing the band on her wrist. 'Domina Pharel always counts them after practice.'

Mina nonchalantly pulls the sleeve of her tunic over it and puts her arms behind her back as if she is stretching. 'I offered to stay and help tidy up, and I slipped one in my belt-purse when she wasn't looking.'

'Oh, Mina. We're not the only class using TASC bands. It's bound to be missed.'

'It's a work-break for the next three days. I'll put it back when I've had a bit of fun.'

'There's always the possibility of not landing where you thought you would,' I warn her.

'I told you, I'm careful. I've only used it to come here. I'm not likely to mis-calibrate in a room this size.'

'You could have landed next door.'

'In Garforth's apartment? Ew.'

'On his bed.' I rub it in.

Mina starts to laugh at the thought of the little nerd in the next room with a female on his bed. My friend's laugh is both raucous and infectious, and I end up with a stitch while Mina is breathless with glee. 'It might give him pause for thought,' she says when she can speak.

'So, you've only used it to come here?' I ask casually.

'Well…'

'Well, what?'

'It has its uses. That…' – she looks me in the eye and raises her forefinger – 'that is all you're getting from me.'

'Dieter,' I say.

'No comment.'

The powers-that-be on this little off-world colony are fairly lenient about male-female relationships among us students as long as it doesn't interfere with the work. Mina and Dieter interfere with everything and so they have been served with restrictions as to when they can see each other and for how long. As all iris scans are monitored, her movements will be logged and she will not be able to visit Dieter without it being known.

'I think you want to be sent home.'

'As if,' she mutters.

'Mina?'

She turns and looks at me. 'What's that tone of voice for?'

'Do yourself a favour and put the TASC band back as soon as you leave here.'

'I can't. The lab's locked until after the work-break.'

'Then leave it with me. Please, Mina.'

'Why should I?'

'I don't want to see you in trouble.'

'You're such a goody-goody, Lottie. Get on with your study. See if I care. I'm off to have some fun.' She pulls up her sleeve and taps at the screen on her wrist. 'It is a work-break, after all.' With a light crackle, she is gone, leaving me feeling very worried.

TASC stands for Time and Space Continuum, and TASC bands are a new invention that has got serious scientists wetting their knickers over what they can help us to achieve. Travel through time as well as space has been feasible for some years, and it's because of this, we humans can explore the universe without fear of dying of old age before we're halfway through the Milky Way. But the machines are too cumbersome and unwieldy for anything other than travel between planets with proper landing bays, and so lots of time and money has been spent on inventing ways of giving individuals a means of hopping about in the Time and Space Continuum without all that irksome and time-consuming programming and finding somewhere to park a machine the size of a rugby stadium.

The TASC band is the size of a wristwatch and designed to be worn as such. As yet it can only be used over short distances and lengths of time, which is great if you're late for that important meeting in a building at the other end of the dome. It is the brainchild of one of the domini here, Dominus Dexter. He must be as old as time itself and is extraordinarily clever. There is a rumour going around that he was in the middle of sex with his wife when he had the idea and leapt up and ran straight to his study to input the formula before he forgot a single digit. How do people know these things? Personally, I don't believe it. I expect someone made it up because Dominus Dexter has no social graces whatsoever, and the fact that he even knows about sex is beyond belief.

Sadly, Domina Dexter died during early trials of the band, but it didn't slow her husband down. The accident made him more intent on perfecting his idea and he worked long hours to make sure it was safe to use before letting it loose on us. By us, I mean the students here in this colony living under a dome on Callirrhoe, a moon of Jupiter.

The TASC band is still a work in progress and that's what worries me the most. Mina is a risk taker. She knows we should only use the band under supervision. She also knows that, as yet, we have very limited data on its efficiency and any effects on the human body, both short and long-term. She could end up anywhere and in any number of pieces if things go horribly wrong.

Convinced that Mina is using the band to sneak into Dieter's room without being seen, I turn back to work; but my friend has worried me and I can't settle. I decide to give up and go and see if anyone I know is about. I might go for a walk to the gardens, sit in the artificial sunlight or chat with friends at the lido. I end up doing nothing of the sort. As I leave my apartment block I bump into a very worried looking Dieter.

'What's she done?' I sigh before he has a chance to speak.

'Come with me, Lottie, please.' He starts to walk away.

'What has she done?'

'I'm saying nothing here,' Dieter hisses out of the corner of his mouth. 'Just come with me. Head for the café and then turn left. Take the second turning and then left again.'

'Where are we going?'

'My place.'

'That's not the way to your place,' I hiss back as I try to keep up with him.

'It is. It's the long way. Slow down. Make it look as if we're going our separate ways. I'll meet you there.' He disappears into the café. I stand for a moment, but there is nothing else to do but follow his directions and take the roundabout route to the block where Dieter lives. There are few people about and all is quiet in the afternoon sun. I wait for a few seconds, but there is no sign of him, so I walk slowly into the block and make my way to his apartment.

The door is locked, but I only have to wait for a couple of minutes before he appears. He eyes the camera screen and unlocks the door, dragging me inside before relocking it swiftly. He slumps into an easy chair. 'She's in the bedroom,' he whispers without giving me eye contact. 'Don't ask. See for yourself.'

I cross the living space and stand sideways on to the bedroom door. It is ajar and I carefully push it open and peer into the gloom. The curtains have been drawn and I have a little difficulty in seeing for a few moments. I can make out Mina's unmistakable red hair spread across the pillow and one arm thrown over the covers. 'Mina?' I am rewarded with a sob.

I move cautiously into the room and stare down at my friend on Dieter's bed. A blanket has been thrown over her in a haphazard fashion and Mina uses the arm I can see to push it to one side.

'Oh, Mina. What have you done?' I sink to my knees beside the bed.

'You've got to help me.'

'What on earth do you expect me to do? Where's the TASC band?'

'On my other arm.'

I pull the blanket fully off of my friend. 'And where's your other arm?'

'I don't know.' Mina bursts into tears.

I sense Dieter by the door, but he doesn't come in.

'Did she appear like this?' I ask.

His shadow nods.

I open my mouth, but Mina pre-empts me. 'Don't say it.'

'Well, I did tell you so. I presume you were aiming for the bedroom?'

'I was aiming for the bed. I thought it would surprise Dee if I suddenly appeared in his bed.'

'Well. You've done that alright!' Now that the initial shock is wearing off I am struggling not to laugh, although that might be hysteria.

'You've got to help me. I'm stuck.' Mina is, indeed, stuck inside the mattress, which would be hilarious if it wasn't so serious.

The TASC band moves a body by breaking it down into its component atoms and then reassembling them at the Arrival Point, or AP for short, that has been programmed in. Since Domina Dexter's accident there have been no others. Certainly, not any we've heard of.

'Are you in pain?'

'No. I can't feel anything. That worries me more.' She's very pale and trembling slightly.

'Well, first we need to find the band. Can you feel your other arm at all?'

She shakes her head. 'I think it's in the bed.'

'What did you programme in? Arrival Point *in* the bed?!' I am being sarcastic, but Mina nods dumbly.

'You idiot,' I say. 'It appears you are now part of Dieter's bed. How do you think I can get you out without the band?'

'Cut the bed open. Find my arm.'

'Don't you bloody dare.' Dieter is still standing in the doorway.

'To be honest, Mina, I think we have to find another TASC band. And, also – I don't think that using it should be left to me or Dieter.'

'It has to be. This is a hanging offence.' I nod at the over exaggeration. 'I'll be expelled in disgrace.' I nod again. 'Don't be so complacent about it.' Mina is all but stage whisper screaming now.

I am not complacent. Mina never pays much attention in lectures because if she did she would be very, very scared right now. If I have interpreted the limited findings of the TASC Experiment right, Mina is now most likely fused with the bed and it will take someone more qualified than a second-year astrophysics student to sort it out.

I move around the bed. I can see her head and upper torso from just below her left shoulder and her left leg from her thigh to her ankle. Her left arm is also free. There is no sign of the rest of her body, her right arm and leg or her left foot. She resembles a surrealistic sculpture

– *Girl in a Bed*. I can't help but snigger. Mina starts to cry. I mean, really cry. I hug her shoulder and then start to squeeze the mattress to see if I can feel any body parts.

'I think we really need to speak to Domina Pharel,' I decide.

'You can't. Please, please, please, please.'

'Alright, but I can't feel anything of you. Do you understand what's happened?'

'No.'

'Perhaps you should listen in lectures. You are now part of the bed. There is nothing I can do. Even if I had a TASC band I would be reluctant to use it in case I made matters worse.' I sit down heavily on the edge of the bed. 'I really think I need to speak to someone who knows what they're doing. Perhaps you'll just have to clean the toilets with a toothbrush for a year or something. They won't use a TASC machine just to send one person home.'

'So where do I stand in all this?' Dieter looks petulant, like a naughty schoolboy. 'I'll be blamed as well. It is my bed.' He folds his arms. 'I'm not being punished for her idiocy.'

What a charming boyfriend! I think, but say, 'You did nothing. We'll both say so.' It wouldn't do to antagonise him when we might need his help.

Mina turns her face to the wall, sobbing all the more.

'OK, OK. I'll try and get hold of another band. Though, goodness knows how I'll manage that.'

'You'll think of something. Say you need something for your work. You have a reputation, use it.' Mina is getting snappy.

'Say to whom?'

'Domina Pharel. The lab will be off limits as it's a work-break. You'll need permission to get in.'

'Bugger you, Mina. She won't give me permission. Not without lots of questions. She'll probably stand over me while I pretend to look for something that isn't there.'

'Pah! You're her blue-eyed girl. She'll probably give you the code.'

'You've got to do it – and quickly.' Dieter is getting more and more anxious. 'I want her out of here.'

I decide they deserve each other as I head for the door – him for his lack of chivalry, her for her sheer stupidity with the TASC band. I am not a good dissembler and, as I make my way to her apartment, I worry about Domina Pharel catching me in the lie. As it happens she barely looks at me. She is still in her dressing gown, flushed and more concerned with something behind her than me.

'Goodness me, Lottie. For heaven's sake take some time off.' She sneaks a furtive glance towards the bedroom. 'Work will wait. Go for a swim or something.' She shuts the door in my face.

Mina is not as rattled as I expect when I tell her. 'You'll have to go through the air ducts,' she tells me matter-of-factly. 'The female toilets are right next door, so it will be easy.'

'OK, so I can get into the lab. How do I get into the safe where the bands are kept?'

'That's easy. I have the code.'

I am incredulous. 'You? Who in their right mind would give you the code?'

'No one. Domina Pharel keeps her safe code in her desk drawer. You should pay more attention to detail sometimes, Lottie.'

I could smack her. 'Won't the drawer be locked?'

'It should be, but I left it open after I helped tidy away. I knew I'd need to put the band back before it was missed.'

'Can't Dieter go?'

'You're not getting me crawling through no bloody tight spaces. I'm claustrophobic.'

'As if,' snaps Mina. 'You just don't want to get dusty.'

'This is really not helping. If you don't stop it, I shall just go home and lock the door. Pretend I don't know you.'

'Sorry. Please do this for me, Lottie. I'll owe you.' She puts on her sweetest smile.

'What can you possibly do for me? You already owe me for last month's research.'

'Aw, Lottie. You're my best friend. Help me out. I can't stay here.'

'No, she bloody can't. What the hell am I going to do?' Dieter is like a petulant toddler.

I sigh deeply and leave them to it. I make my way to the block housing the teaching laboratories and let myself in. That is the easy part as the library is open at all times for students and Domini alike. It is silent and gloomy inside, and the sudden flicker as the lights are activated by my presence makes me jump. The light sensors are so much a way of life I had forgotten that they will light the building up when no one is supposed to be in. I make for the library and am relieved to find it empty. If anyone was there, I was going to say I was there for a disk or restricted information.

There is no one present at all, not even a janitor, so, after a few seconds of indecision, I make my way to the toilets on the first floor.

The grill covering the air duct on the wall is easily removable by sliding the blade of my nail file behind the flat edge and popping the fastenings. I lay it carefully in the nearest cubicle, out of sight of a cursory glance. I pull myself up, thanking the powers-that-be for insisting we keep ourselves physically fit. The airway is pristine, but then it wouldn't do for us to be breathing grubby microbes.

It doesn't take long to slide along to the grill in the laboratory next door. I push at it and it moves far too easily, clattering to the floor. I hide my head in my arms, expecting the sirens to start, but nothing happens. I lay for as long as it takes for my trembling to subside enough to allow me to do something and then let myself carefully down into the lab. I begin to wish I had used the loo before I climbed up here.

The code is in the drawer, just as Mina said it would be, and I tap it into the keypad on the door of the safe. There are five bands inside. I take one and close the door quietly before heading back to the vent.

Now I know why everything has gone so smoothly. I haven't thought about how I am going to replace the grill with me inside the duct. I swear at Mina under my breath as I look around for something I can use to hook the grill from high up. The lab has been cleared for the break. There is not so much as a stylus lying about. I sit on the floor with my back to the wall and think. I open my belt purse in order to hide the band when an idea occurs to me. I can use the strap of my belt purse. If I link it through the grill, I can draw it up after me and wedge it into place.

The first part of the plan works well enough, but I have great difficulty in snapping the fastenings closed. I manage two and hope that it will hold. Rethreading my belt purse, I slide back to the toilets and clamber down, replacing the grill with ease.

My first thought as I open the outside door to leave the teaching labs is *I'm glad I used the toilet before I left.* The second is *Fuck you, Mina.* I didn't even consider that I could have used the TASC band to get me to Dieter's apartment.

Domina Pharel's expression is inscrutable, as are the faces of the two security officers standing behind her. She holds out her hand and I fumble in my belt purse and draw out the band, placing it carefully in her palm. She tuts sadly before turning away.

The guards obviously have their orders and they escort me silently back to my apartment.

The jumble of incoherent thoughts in my head immobilises me. I am mortified, mortified at appearing so untrustworthy before Domina Pharel and mortified that I let Mina talk me into doing what I did. I am distraught, worried that I'm likely to be sent home. I sit at my little kitchen table, aware of the security guards outside of my door. If asked, I will tell the truth – I think. I don't like the thought of telling on my friend, but I won't be able to help her if I don't.

Afternoon has given way to evening when the door to my apartment opens and Domina Pharel and the head of security, Chief Sandor, walk in. They sit opposite me without a word and Chief Sandor opens her notebook. She inserts a lead in the port at the rear and looks expectantly at me.

I have never been questioned before and stare blankly at her.

'She wants your right index finger,' Domina Pharel says tonelessly.

I offer the finger to the head of security and she clips the other end of the lead over the end. She taps the notebook. 'Full name?'

'Charlotte Brown.'

'Date of birth?'

'Earth date twenty-one, twelve, twenty-two, twelve.'

'Date of arrival on Callirrhoe D1?'

'Earth date, One, one, twenty-two, twenty-one.'

Chief Sandor nods to her colleague. It is a signal for Domina Pharel to take over the questioning.

'Why did you let Minerva Atkins talk you into breaking the colony rules?'

I had to think for a minute. Mina hates her name and is never referred to as Minerva unless she's in trouble. Which, of course, she is.

'How is she?'

'Why did you let her talk you into it?'

I feel a tear roll down my cheek. 'Am I to go home?'

'Why did you let her talk you into it?' Insistent.

'She's my friend.' Domina Pharel's expression says *some friend*. 'I told her it would be better if I spoke to you. I couldn't help her.'

'But, still, you stole the band.'

I shrug. 'I wouldn't have used it.'

'But, still, you stole the band.'

I hang my head. I have no excuse that doesn't sound trite so say nothing.

Looking at Chief Sandor, who nods her head almost imperceptibly, Domina Pharel sighs and stands. 'How could you think we wouldn't know?' she asks. 'The plate the bands sit on is a scale that monitors the weight of what it is holding. As soon as you lifted a band security was warned. We were already monitoring Minerva.'

She waits for an answer, but I have nothing.

'Can I trust you to stay in your apartment for now?'

I nod.

'Anything you need will be brought to you.'

I swallow and nod again. I hear the door shut and lay my head on the table and break my heart as the darkness deepens.

Eventually, I have to answer a call of nature and decide to shower away the afternoon while I'm up. Dressed only in a towel, I go into the bedroom for clean clothes, only to be stopped in my tracks. In the gloom, I see a hump in my bed. Cautiously I slide towards it and, taking a deep breath, fling back the sheets to find that the mattress has developed a right hip while I've been busy.

Without thinking, I rush through the outside door and out onto the landing to find Garforth in urgent conversation with a guard. He colours beautifully at the sight of me in a towel and falls to stammering. The guard, bless him, ushers us into my apartment.

'Get dressed.' He points towards the bedroom and I obey. When I return, he and Garforth are sitting at my table with a mug of coffee each and one waiting for me.

'Where?' A man of few words. I point to the bedroom and he steps sprightly in. On his return, he opens his unique cell, or UC for short, and passes the information on to the powers-that-be.

Within minutes the block is swarming with guards and two beds are manhandled into the lift and out of the building. Before we have time to take it all in, Garforth and I are left alone with cooling cups of rather bad coffee.

I make tea this time and we sit and wait.

'What did *you* find?' I ask eventually.

'A foot.' Garforth gulps at his tea. 'It was horrible. I could see the toes sticking up when I pulled back the sheet.' He stops and stares at me. 'They were wiggling.' He breathes, eyes wide with horror.

I start to giggle. I can't stop.

'Are you alright?' he asks.

I shake my head. I most definitely am not alright. The giggles turn to tears. I can't see this ever being put right.

No one comes near that night, nor the next day. I stay put as I promised but begin to get more and more frustrated by the lack of communication.

Eventually, on the last day of the work-break Domina Pharel and Chief Sandor knock at my door. I take it as a good sign. I imagine they would have just barged in if I was too deeply in the mire.

'Perhaps you'd like to make some tea, Charlotte.' They sit at my little table without being invited, which I take as a retrograde step. Sandor gets out her notebook without looking at me. I do as I am asked and when we are all sitting with steaming mugs of tea Domina Pharel addresses me.

'You should have reported Minerva as soon as you knew.'

I nod dumbly. 'I know. I did come to you first.' She colours. 'But she's my friend. How is she?'

'How do you think?'

'Have you found all her parts?' I grimace at my own words. I'm making her sound like an android.

'I'm afraid not. I doubt we will.'

I gasp at the thought of it. Mina is conscious of what is going on. I cannot imagine how she must be feeling. 'What will happen now?'

'To you?'

'To Mina.'

'That's for us to know. As for you...' My vision tunnels and I hear my blood rushing in my ears. I stare at my tutor in fear. 'You are a very promising student and you didn't use the band. I am reluctant to send you home. Minerva has insisted she forced you into it, although...' She doesn't finish. I look at her expectantly. 'I imagine you have learnt a hard lesson?' I nod vigorously. 'And Mina will no longer be around to coerce you into anything.'

I wait, my heart pounding. 'We have decided that you can stay but...' She pauses for effect. 'You will have to accept sanctions.'

'Of course,' I whisper.

'You will be taken off the TASC course.' A tear escapes. I love that course, despite the dangers. 'You will be reassigned as my personal assistant.' That wasn't so bad. I can learn a lot from the Domina. It just means my leisure time will be restricted – very restricted. 'I also expect straight As in all of your assignments. If you achieve that, we will review a year from today.'

'Thank you, Domina. I don't deserve that.'

'No, you don't. But, then you don't deserve to be sent home in disgrace either. We both lose out that way.' She and the Chief get up and head for the door. 'Seven o'clock sharp in my lab, please, Student Brown. We'll see ourselves out.'

The door has barely finished rattling in its frame when I hear a timid tap. On opening it, I find Garforth standing there wearing a knowing grin and carrying chocolate cake. I drag him in. He's not so bad once you get to know him.

THE SOUVENIR

Nick Marsh

'Is it one of ours?' asked Berri.

'I don't recognise… My god, it's ancient!' exclaimed Cavall, zooming up on the screen.

For a moment the two voyagers focused on the screen, occasionally looking up to see the unidentified craft through the window. Cavall manipulated the thrusters, reducing the closing rate to what seemed like walking speed. 'Plenty of time, plenty of time,' he repeated, as if anticipating a comment from his colleague.

It was almost half an hour before the craft filled the window. 'A little rotation – ten or twenty degrees?' queried Berri.

'Yep, fine. Cancel on—'

'I know,' Berri cut him off. She turned the ship, and as it stabilised Cavall flicked on the tracking lock. Now they could both enjoy the view.

'I just… I just can't believe it,' Berri said, looking at the strange mixture of bright reflective surfaces and the dark, jagged edges of twisted metal. 'Where do you think it's from?'

'You're the archaeologist,' smiled Cavall. 'But I'd say it's a long way from home. A very long way.'

'It is truly…' Berri sought the right word.

'Old? Knackered?' Cavell offered.

'How can you be so bloody blasé about it?'

'What makes you think I'm blasé?'

'You… oh, I don't know! I'll start my report.'

'Plenty of time, as I keep telling you. If this is a historic moment, then let's look on and soak it up. If I'm blasé, perhaps it's my way of trying to take in the situation.'

For the next few minutes the two space voyagers floated shoulder to shoulder, looking out on the only other constructed object for billions of miles. It was certainly ancient, the main cylindrical hull being pockmarked from thousands of miniscule collisions of the sort that, in interstellar space, might only occur once every hundred years. Interestingly, the craft was gathered in two main sections, held together by what seemed little more than sheet metal. It was junk, junk of the kind that even a scrap merchant might shrug his shoulders at. But it was space junk. And it was completely unidentifiable.

Berri switched on her microphone. '201/3652 Expedition 603. Report 211. Object in visual range. Unidentified, repeat unidentified. Cylindrical body, approximately two hundred and fifty metres with interconnecting struts two-thirds down. Reaction nozzles visible at far end. Broken section at top end, probably once part of same structure. No definable shape. Significant damage. Surfaces exceptionally scarred. Other broken sections splayed out, some possibly in local orbit. Age unknown. If damage caused by debris field, estimate a few hundred years. If craft tracked through clear space…' Berri paused.

Cavall, in the meantime, had also started his report. He continued as Berri fell silent. 'Craft tumbling at rate of one revolution – with combined rolling motion – every twenty-two minutes. No identifier. No detectable transmissions. Colour dull grey with spilling black internals. Some glass but overall metal-alloy structure. Collision damage all over but some inscriptions and part of a blue insignia on main cylinder – camera to confirm. Visible propulsion – ancient chemical rocketry. Doubtful galactic capability. Limited living space unless alien life-form exceptionally small.'

Berri looked at Cavall; he'd said the 'A' word. He returned her glance with uncharacteristic awkwardness.

'Do you…?' asked Berri.

'I'm not able to come up with any other conclusion. Yes. Yes, of course. It must be. Prime reason for the founding of the Galactic Exploration Group. Not to mention the whole bloody history of exploration since the Founding Fathers.'

Berri started to laugh.

'What? What is it?!' Cavall protested, a little irritated at her reaction.

'I've never seen you like this. It's ridiculous. You're ridiculous!'

'Gee, thanks! Why don't you get your report finished and send it off with mine while I prepare for a spacewalk?'

'You're not letting me—?'

'Berri, it's both procedure and it's sensible for only one of us to go out there to make sure it's safe. And as the Captain it's my call, and I'm doing it.'

Berri bit her lip. Cavall turned and started to download the checklist. Was he really concerned about her safety or just pulling rank? No doubt he was thinking of his place in history. Procedure – how she hated the word!

An hour later, Berri was monitoring the thrusters as the airlock hissed and Cavall came into view. For a moment he span around in the void like a disorientated diver, performing checks and ensuring the connection on the tethering cable. This was a true spacewalk – or flight, to be more accurate. With a booster on his back and a hand booster attached to each wrist, Cavall had full movement control. The tether was merely a backup or means of retrieval should the unthinkable happen.

Eventually Cavall blipped the back booster and shot towards the craft. His glinting, new spacesuit quickly receded, and it was only then that Berri appreciated the scale of the alien craft. She switched on the laser scanners – a full model would be necessary, particularly in this, its pre-retrieval condition.

Berri saw the flashes from the hand boosters as Cavall slowed himself onto the craft. He'd aimed for the break point where, all of a sudden, the fragile bits of connecting metal and threads of cable seemed hazardous to the tiny figure in their midst. Berri watched closely as Cavall manoeuvred himself in the debris, then saw that he was guiding himself along a twisted beam. 'Be careful! You said this was only a spacewalk. What's the radiation level?'

'Negative radiation. Craft is long dead.'

'Are you going to look at the other side?'

'Not yet. It'll come into view as the craft tumbles round again. I'm going in.'

'Cavall, you are not going in. Repeat, you are not to enter! Rule twenty-one of the—'

'For God's sake Berri, I wrote that code! The path is clear. From this angle there is a large void and it's easy have a peek inside.'

'Do not go in, Cavall. Do not go in!'

'Out of transmission' sounded the Communications Controller.

'Damn the arrogant fool!' hissed Berri, slapping the desk.

For what seemed like ages, Berri watched in silence. Thoughts of reporting to Mission Control filled her mind. Had she done all she could to prevent his recklessness? Had she and Cavall been the melded team they'd presented themselves to be before the selection committee? How had she got his back up?

But the man was always so distant. And so patronising – even within the first few hours of the mission. What was it, Berri wondered, that made experienced flyers look on field experts like her with such disdain?

And yet, why was she not elated? The find was unbelievable – and to think they had only noticed the radar image a few hours before. The situation was unprecedented. At any one time, the GEG had up to seventy expeditionary craft on missions and never had one of them come across something like this. In its whole four hundred and sixty-two years, Mission Control's only evidence of alien life had been the Larvey transmission of over a century ago. Now the experts were pouring cold water over even that one. Berri stared intently at the alien craft – perhaps it had just been something experimental, a secret covered up by the Founding Fathers, something that had been deleted from the annals of history.

'—like a quadruped! Whoah! I need to get my breath!'
    'Cavall! Cavall – can you hear me?'
    'Loud and clear, Berri. Did you catch that?'
    'No, you've just come back into range. Are you OK?'

'Er, yes. All systems – yes. I was just describing what was in there.'

'Dead or alive?'

'Dead. Long dead, thankfully. But they gave me a shock. Two of them.'

'Oxygen is low.'

'Thanks. I'll come back immediately and tell you everything over a hot drink. Should have some good video shots.'

An hour later saw Cavall and Berri sipping Effer and scrutinising the large screen. 'Once I passed the twisted metal, I found myself in this space.' Cavall pointed. 'Just look at these ancient switches and indication screens – some are still intact!'

'My goodness! Not dissimilar from the controls on Voyager 2 – four hundred years ago!'

'But this craft is much older. And it's only a local ship. I doubt it went further than the local moons. It must have taken millennia to get here. Watch as I go round this corner.'

'Shit! That's one of them, isn't it?'

'I'd expected it but, my goodness, Berri, I nearly filled my spacesuit. I just kept telling myself that it was dead.'

'Is that its skin – grey?'

'No – its suit. And I guess it wasn't originally that colour. It looks floppy but the body inside has rotted away, even in these almost-sterile conditions. Perhaps there was an accident.'

'The collision that ripped the craft in half?'

'I reckon that came later. Now have a look at this – the rounded head is actually a suit helmet, not unlike ours. It's fronted by glass, too. Watch as I get the courage to wipe the surface.'

'Ugh! I think I'm going to be sick!'

'It's just the remaining imprint of its biology – you can guess that! In life I doubt it looked anything like that. Think of our skeletons. I daresay if I'd knocked it, the dust would have fallen away completely.'

'Hey! There's that insignia again. On the spacesuit!'

'You're right. If only we knew its meaning.'

A few hours later, Berri woke to see Cavall up and bent over the communications desk. She released herself from the bed and floated over to see what was up. 'Morning,' she said, as cheerfully as she could manage.

'Have a look at this,' said Cavall. 'Came from Expedition Control an hour ago.'

Berri read the transmission. 'They've got to be joking?!'

'General Corder himself. The old fool.'

'But "destroy completely"? Did they not read our communications? Don't they realise that this is the greatest find in the history of space exploration – the greatest find ever! – possibly the only evidence of life outside our cluster. What the hell are they playing at? The pictures alone would have people queuing for miles!'

'Calm down, Berri.'

'I can't calm down! I won't calm down! And you, you cultural moron, I suppose you're going to obey the order? Don't tell me, you've already planned the best way of doing it! You and your bloody procedures!'

'Berri wait! Just let me speak!'

'Bloody flyers – you have no idea!' Berri sprung forwards and started pounding Cavall with her fists. 'It was just as bad at university! How can scientists ever get it into your thick skulls… that… that…' Slowly Berri slumped into a foetal position.

'Sorry, Berri,' Cavall said, withdrawing the needle. 'It's for your own good.'

Berri woke to see Cavall bent over the Communications desk. Was this déjà vu? No, this time Cavall was in the spacesuit. 'Why… why can't I move?' she strained.

Cavall turned and smiled awkwardly. He moved over to her. 'Berri, I'm glad to see you're alright.'

'But, what the hell?!'

'Berri, just listen.'

'Don't tell me it's for my own good.'

'It's for your own good.' He smiled, almost apologetically. 'I had to drug you. You were a potential danger. Now, here's the situation and I want you to hear me out before making any comments, OK?'

'I don't have a lot of choice, do I?'

'Expedition Control received our reports and I can only guess that they have been fully digested.'

'But why…?'

'They expressed a concern for the fledgling planet Xenar which, as you know, is not far away. Our position and trajectory information, combined with estimations of the masses of the alien craft and the planet, indicate that the craft might be caught in orbit, albeit a very distant and elliptical one.'

'What?!'

'I know, it's a clutching at straws, but there is a small chance that one day, perhaps in a few millennia, the craft will impact Xenar and contaminate it.'

'But—?'

'Let me finish. Believe me, I know I'm a "thick-skulled flyer" but I've probably covered the questions you're going to ask. The Expedition Committee judge Xenar to be of prime importance in the Development and Colonisation Project, and even though the alien craft has negligible radiation, it may have surviving microbial life.'

'But, retrieval?'

'Is the other thing. Again, microbial contamination of one of our home planets cannot be ruled out. An orbital location is possible, but transportation would be difficult and there would be the constant threat of unauthorised access.'

'So we destroy!'

'Berri, I'm going to tell you this once and you're going to listen. Then, although it is strictly against procedure with you in this condition, I'm about to entrust you with my life. As captain I have the unique code for crew restraint. Your locks are timed to release in an hour. By that time, I will be outside fixing a nuclear mine onto the alien craft. You will take charge of the ship and open the airlock for my return. What you actually choose to do will be up to you, but I will set the mine's timer for two hours with no external override. It will therefore destroy the craft, whatever fate you decide for me or this spaceship.'

Berri stared at Cavall. Had he really said what she thought he'd said? The fate of the alien craft was of prime importance, but the situation had taken a sinister turn. But, for the time being, there was nothing she could do.

The next hour was possibly the longest of Berri's life. At last there was a buzzing noise and her limbs flopped outwards. Automatically she headed for the control station and looked through the main window. At first she couldn't see Cavall, but then she noticed a flash from behind the alien craft and an object accelerating rearwards. No – two objects, the first one a rocket and the following one seemingly unpropelled, but much larger and orange in colour.

'Cavall, can you hear me?'

'Shit! Yes, loud and clear. Don't tell me an hour's up?'

'Is everything alright?'

'Think so. I'm coming back. Can you prepare the airlock?'

'Of course.'

'I'm just on the hand boosters. The flight may be erratic.'

Cavall's return was indeed erratic, though few would have managed it as well as he. Each blip of a hand booster sent him spinning and going off at an odd angle until finally he stabilised himself about fifty metres from the entrance and drifted in at a crawl.

'Oxygen low, Cavall.'

'I know.'

'So what was all that about?' asked Berri, helping Cavall out of the spacesuit.

'All what about?'

'You know,' she smiled.

'As you know,' Cavell whispered, 'we're on permanent Mission Record mode. Maybe one day.' He smiled at her. 'Right, set a course for Lunar Base 3 and give it full thrust!' He glanced at the clock. 'Fifty-one minutes to nuclear detonation and there's no drag in space!'

Thirty-two days later, Berri was sitting in a café on the downtown side of Mission Control. Ten or so years ago, this had been one of her favourite hangouts, where she would rendezvous with friends after a week's training and look down on the city over a cup or two of the bar's own special brew. It was comfortably out of the zone frequented by the many young hopefuls trying to get their wings on elementary orbital cruisers.

The café was on one of the last floors of a high rise block and, although the roof was equipped with a landing pad, the place was sufficiently cheap and dingy to deter any visitors of worth. This included journalists, the like of whom Berri had been avoiding since returning from her recent mission.

She sipped the hot Effer and looked out across the city to the launch pads thirty miles away. The location gave an excellent view of launches and was probably the city's best kept secret.

'Anyone sitting here?'

'Cavall! What the hell are you doing?'

'Heard this was your favourite hangout. Funny, I used to come here myself when I was a student.'

'So, are we safe? Have things been quiet?'

'Quiet for the moment. The Expedition Committee is still managing to keep a clamp on things. But it'll get out sure enough. Just a matter of time. Perhaps you should book a holiday on Lunar Base 2?'

'Why Lunar 2?'

'Precisely.'

'Is it safe to talk?'

'As safe as anywhere and I doubt if it'll matter either way. General Corder's on gardening leave. Between you and me, he and a few other committee members might be facing a trial sometime in the future.'

'So we are safe?'

'Not yet. In fact, they could have me for breaking a principal article. As you know, the discovery of alien life was one of the stated aims of the Founding Fathers.'

'But you were obeying direct orders.'

'Yes, I was, wasn't I?'

'It's still intact, isn't it?'

'What on earth could you mean by that?' laughed Cavall. 'Don't I always stick to procedures? Like every uncultured moron of a flyer!'

'I'm sorry,' said Berri. 'I just couldn't get over the importance of the find.'

'And you were right not to. That's what I like about you. I've just been playing the game too long.'

'But you risked your life by using your booster pack to shift the nuclear mine. I doubt if anyone else could have made it back to the ship on hand boosters alone. Though you did look funny.'

'It was the only idea I could come up with. By the time it exploded, that mine would have been nearly two thousand miles away. Even so, the blast has probably damaged that ancient bit of wreckage. At least Mission Control detected the explosion.'

'But we have the co-ordinates and…'

'When there's a change of blood at Expedition Control. Maybe then they'll let you go and have a good nose around. Until then don't go mentioning it to anyone.'

'So how old was it?'

'Have a guess, Miss First-Class Archaeologist. I'm just back from the lab, unofficially of course.'

'Two thousand… Five thousand years?'

'Between one hundred thousand and a few million.'

'Phewwww!'

51

'Of course the evidence is still under wraps, but I have an old friend in the lab who hasn't slept a wink since we returned.'

'What about text translations? How about that funny blue insignia; was that text?'

'Funny you should mention that,' smiled Cavell, reaching into his pocket.

Berri watched intently as he opened his hand to reveal a piece of metal bent into the shape of a circle. 'The blue insignia!'

'Strictly against procedure, of course, but while I was inside I ripped this from one of the spacesuits. Don't worry, I've had it checked out. It's sterile and quite inert. Personally, I think it's some sort of bonding or love symbol – the characters are simple and almost symmetrical.'

'But why is it bent into a ring shape?'

'For someone to wear, dear Berri.'

'You stupid old fool!'

'Another one to add to the list!'

Berri stared intently at the ring. It was just a piece of space junk, but millions of years old and from a race that were probably no more. The insignia was beautiful: NASA.

'Will you wear it for me?' asked Cavall.

'Is this your way of proposing, or just another procedure, Commander Cavall?' And, with a smile, Berri offered the middle of her three fingers.

SafeChip™

MM Schreier

Thea's SafeChip™ hadn't been working when it happened.

Three rapid blinks should have launched the ocular recording module. When her fear spiked, an automatic trouble ticket should have been filed with local law enforcement. As her heart raced and the pain tore through her, a first response team should have been dispatched to her GPS location.

None of that happened.

With the advent of SafeChip™ New York had become the safest city in the world. There was no reason why Thea shouldn't have taken the shortcut through the alley. She was in a rush to meet friends for lunch and had gone that way a hundred times before.

She had known her implant was faulty, but making an appointment to get it repaired was such a hassle. Refabrication and testing could take an entire cycle and Thea was busy with her new teaching job. It wasn't that big of a deal – she didn't really need the Health and Security apps. She was young and hearty. Violent crime was nonexistent, a thing of long-forgotten folklore. It was law that all citizens maintained a functional chip and she had every intention of getting it repaired. It just hadn't seemed that urgent.

Until the incident.

Rough hands slammed her against the side of the building and her skull bounced off brick with a resounding thunk. Stunned, she struggled to focus. His leer swam in her vision, crowded with stained and crooked teeth. It was a hell of a thing to notice, but everyone had perfect smiles these days. Perfect skin. Perfect hair. Beauty was a programmed standard, enchanting features chosen à la carte from a menu of model-like ideals.

Shock eclipsed the bite of the knife sinking into Thea's stomach. Things like that just didn't happen. It was unbelievable, and her brain was having trouble processing the sensation. Her body caught up when he pulled the blade out and the agony consumed her.

Blink. Blink. Blink.

Thea screamed when she realized that no one was coming.

Her field of view narrowed to a pinpoint. His twisted sneer was the last thing she saw before the world went dark.

A rhythmic beeping intruded on Thea's dreams. She didn't want to wake. It was safe swimming through the warm seascape of blurred thought. A never-ending present buoyed her, sheltered her from her memories.

A wave of sound pulled at her, dragging her toward the surface. The swell shattered into fragments of whispered conversation. The disjointed phrases jabbed at her, icy shards pricking her consciousness.

…unknown stomach laceration…lost a lot of blood… SafeChip™ seems nonfunctional…lucky a passerby found her… will have questions…highly unusual…

Thea's eyes fluttered open. The hospital bed was tucked in a stark room, walls painted an immaculate bleach-white. The monochrome purity bothered her; its pristine brilliance felt like an illusion. An IV tethered her to the dinging, flashing machinery. She sucked in a deep breath that tasted like antiseptic. Even that much movement was a mistake. Pain stabbed her side. The bleeping became a jangled, insistent squalling.

"Try not to move." The voice was clipped, bright but lacking in depth. Its owner, a middle-aged man in an impeccable charcoal suit, sat stiff-backed in the unyielding plastic visitor's chair. His blonde hair was trimmed stylishly short. "You've been through quite an ordeal." He grinned, thin lips pulled back from pearly, even teeth. The smile wasn't friendly.

Thea's heart thumped and the beeping mirrored her distress.

"My name is Agent Willis, from the Department of Anomalies." With a practiced flip of the wrist he flashed a shiny badge. "Can you tell me what happened?" The man's eyes were jewel green and just as hard.

Thea swallowed. The words stuck in her throat. Would he believe her?

"I know this is difficult, Miss Martinez." He reached out and patted her arm.

Thea jerked away. Being touched by a stranger made her skin crawl. She wondered if she'd ever feel safe again.

The agent narrowed his eyes. "Tell me what happened."

The stern command unlocked her voice. Words tumbled from her in a chaotic jumble. Small details were frighteningly vivid. The shade of the alley had felt cool on her face after the blazing heat of the afternoon sun. The man's hands had been weathered and his face creased with wrinkles. Not aged. Worn. His dark eyes glittered, almost feverish. Their intensity had sliced as deep as the knife. His breath stank of whiskey and desperation.

"He laughed when he... stabbed me." Thea stumbled over the unfamiliar word. "I'm sorry. It's all so surreal." She couldn't remember if her purse had fallen from numb fingers or if he had yanked it from her grasp. She choked back a sob. "Why me? Why did I have to be the first... victim... in hundreds of years?" Her history degree was serving her well. Without it she wouldn't have had the words to define the experience.

Willis snorted, his lips twitching. The sound brought Thea up short. The agent rolled his eyes. "Please." His voice was mocking. "Everyone's a victim. You pathetic *sheep* just don't remember."

Thea wracked her brain trying to make sense of the comment. Sheep – a domesticated ruminant animal with a thick woolly coat that had been raised for meat and fiber. Extinct. No, wrong context. Sheep – a person who is too easily influenced or led. Her stomach flipped.

"Ah. A glimmer of understanding?" Willis's laugh was condescending. "It's the SafeChip™ of course. Keeps the population compliant." His eyes were flat and cold. "Violent crime is worse than ever. Makes the 21st century look like utopia. Your implants rewrite your memories." He winked. "It saves us millions on police investigations. Eradicates the nuisance of social justice warriors."

Heat swept through Thea, red hot outrage. She sat up,

but was yanked short. It took a moment for her to realize that she was handcuffed to the bed-rail.

"Don't worry." Agent Willis fiddled with a knob on the IV. "Your implant will be repaired by the morning. You won't remember any of this… unpleasantness." He gave her a wolfish smirk.

A wave of dizziness washed over Thea, and she slumped back on the pillows. Willis's toothy smile was the last thing she saw before sleep took her.

A rhythmic beeping intruded on Thea's dreams. Eyelids flickering, she fought against the sticky cobwebs of slumber. The nightmare was fading, slipping through her fingers like sugar-fine sand.

Thea's head throbbed and her side echoed it in a dull, persistent ache. An IV tethered her to the dinging machinery. Her thoughts were muddled. A sense of déjà vu plagued her and she reached up to rub her temples.

"Easy now." A gentle hand touched her shoulder. She glanced up, and a tall man dressed in scrubs smiled down at her. His brown eyes were warm and encouraging. "Try not to move too much."

"What happened?" Thea remembered a sharp pain in her stomach, then the world had gone black.

The nurse's voice was a deep, soothing baritone. "You collapsed on the sidewalk. The first response team arrived just in time. We had to perform an emergency appendectomy."

A trickle of fear ran through Thea and she reached out to grab the man's hand. He squeezed back.

"Get some rest. You'll feel better in the morning. I say this all the time, but that implant saved your life today." He fiddled with a knob on the IV and left the room.

Thea snuggled into the pillows, eyelids heavy. A wave of gratitude washed through her. How lucky they all were to have the SafeChip™. Her lips curled up in a smile as she drifted off into a safe and dreamless sleep.

RIBBON WORLD

Cathy Hemsley

G ant pushed the calculations and drawings for the
new light sensors aside. He needed fresh air and
fresh ideas. He grabbed his thickest cloak, ruffled his fur
against the cold and went out onto his flat roof. The sun
was a flaming sliver against the pale green sky. At least he
could see it, unlike the poor folk further darkside. He
tapped his imager on and magnified the sliver of light.
Nearly there, he said to himself, nearly enough money in
the bank to move closer to the Meridian suburbs and
have a little more heat.

From here, he could see the masts, gantries and wires
of the water purification plant. The control lights were
flashing as usual. Gant watched for a while then nodded
in satisfaction. It was operating normally. No need to go
in. He turned to breathe in the chill wind from the
darkside.

A bright dot of light caught his attention as it appeared
against the deep-green turbulent clouds. Gant had never
seen any lights that far out. He stared at it as it sprinted
across the clouds deeper into the dark, hung for an
instant, then suddenly dropped. It faded to a glimmer. He
looked around. No one else was visible. This far darkside
it was too cold for people to linger outside.

Gant pointed the imager towards the glimmer and turned it to max. It looked like a slider or vehicle of some sort, but it was too far away for him to be sure. Whatever it was, it had travelled unbelievably fast. And if there was anyone in it, they would not survive long out there. It might have gone off course. It might have crashed.

Gant ran down the house steps, got into his slider and rode the rail to the edge of the settlement. At the end of the rail he flicked on the lights and hovered to feed the coordinates from the imager into the nav. Then he set off at maximum power over the scrubby faig bushes, rocks and frost-covered shrivelled grasses towards the distant gleam.

The slider climbed up a craggy slope, between snow-filled crevices, to a windswept plateau. Gant squinted through the gloom and could make out a large unlighted vehicle. He drove closer, between the tumbled folds of rock, drifts of snow and frost-covered boulders. In the glare from his slider lights, he saw that it was bigger than any vehicle he'd ever seen. Its body was a grey ovoid marked with strange red symbols. It had steering fins and vast dark funnels. Jets, he realised. The snow and ice crystals strewn across the plateau had melted into dark pools of water around its base. As he got out of his slider, the freezing wind howled and stung through his cloak and fur. His nostril hairs crackled with cold as his breath swirled in clouds around his face.

A hatch in the huge ovoid flipped open, a pale light shone from inside, and a figure came out, carrying a box and with cases slung round its shoulders. It walked slowly down a ramp towards him. It was extremely tall and thin – abnormally thin, almost emaciated – and was dressed in close-fitting white overalls of leather-like material and a helmet with a visor that covered its face. The bitter cold air swept huge white snowflakes around it. Gant shivered.

The figure – the woman? Gant assumed she was female from her height – stopped, looked at him and paused. Then she pulled something from her belt and pointed it at the ground near Gant's feet. It had a metal nozzle and looked like a gun or weapon of some sort. Gant stood still. His comms glove flickered a warning light, but he didn't need to see it to know that his heartbeat was raised. He could tap out the emergency code without her seeing him, he thought, but he hesitated.

'I mean… no harm. Peaceful… will you… help me…' she said in a faltering and distorted voice that he could barely hear over the roar of the wind and the deep humming coming from her vehicle.

'Who are you? What do you want?' Gant asked.

'Many things… shelter… water… important… must be secret. Help… shelter… Can you?'

Gant noticed her hands. They were bare of fur. The fingers were elongated as if they'd been stretched and her second thumbs were missing. He wondered what had happened to her. Maybe she was a soldier from the border war with Hyron who'd been captured, tortured and starved, then escaped somehow.

'Alright. Get in,' Gant said, pointing towards the slider.

At his house-cube, the stranger collapsed into a chair. Gant fetched water and some dried fiag fruits and craen biscuits, but the food was pushed aside.

'No… too risky,' she said and took her helmet off.

Gant sat down, open-mouthed. All the fur was missing from her face, like the skincheeks in the heatside slums who shaved their faces. A ridge of flesh split her nostril into two oval holes and a thin grey tube ran from one, along her narrow face and inside her collar. Despite her height, the face wasn't female. Male, not female then, Gant decided.

'Who are you?' Gant stuttered. 'Where are you from?'

She, or rather he, spoke, but it sounded like garbled nonsense. He shook his head and flicked at a silver button on a patch on his shoulder. 'Translator,' he said. 'Not fast... not good... will manage. I am Sorin.' There was a slight delay between his lips moving and the mechanical sound of his voice.

'Sorin, I'm Gant. Are you...' he hesitated. 'Are you male or female?'

'What?... I am male. So you are... Gant. Male? Female?'

'Male.'

'Oh... So... Talk slowly. Translator will... learn. Good. Water...'

Sorin pulled something from a case and thrust it into the glass. It beeped. A probe, Gant thought. Sorin drank.

'Good. I needed water. I need help too. If you will,' he said.

'I will,' Gant said.

'That is good. So... This is the... arrangement. I stay here secretly. You teach me... explain... show... I need to gather information. Will offer... trade... in return...'

'Why? Who for? Are you from Hyron? Or Fialto? How did you get out there? So far darkside? And your transport, what is it? It is not a slider. I've never seen anything like it.'

'Slower… No, not from those places. I will have to tell you… but must be secret…' He paused for a moment, tapping his fingers on the table. Then, looking steadily at Gant, he said, 'I am from another sun. A star.'

'What! That's incredible!'

Gant had, of course, heard of the discoveries of other suns, the 'stars', that existed unseen above the heatside glare and darkside clouds. He knew of the vast receivers on a high mountain deep in the heatside that listened for sounds from these other stars, of the satellites in orbit that mapped and photographed the vast cosmos around their planet, of the speculation about other life on unknown planets – but that was just speculation.

'But… but they are too far away!' he stuttered.

'Yes. Five light cycles away,' Sorin said. 'With… quantum photon jets, it has taken me fifteen cycles to get here.'

'Fifteen cycles? That's impossible. You cannot be telling the truth. From the stars, travelling for fifteen cycles? The oldest person we know of has only survived three. I don't understand.'

'It is true. That is how long it took. Perhaps a translator mistake? Your cycles, the time to go round your sun, may be… greater than mine. No matter… You have to believe me.'

He pulled out his gun and pointed it at Gant, who stared back at him open-mouthed.

'Back to the arrangement… You help. You keep my arrival, where I am from, secret. Tell no one.'

'Why? Why the secrecy?'

'There are reasons… I cannot explain. My government needs information before being… being known about. May trade with you. You help, or…'

'Or what?'

'I kill you,' Sorin replied simply, nodding towards his gun. 'I find someone else.'

Gant leaned back and stared at the other. It was hard to think kindly of someone who had a gun pointed at you, but Sorin *was* ugly. His mouth and teeth were flattened, his ears too large and low, and he had a strange, bony protuberance above his two nostrils. It was almost possible to believe that he came from another world. Gant thought of the strange transport and how it had flown across the sky and dropped to the ground, unlike any other transport he knew. Sorin could be telling the truth.

'Put your weapon away,' Gant said. 'You don't need to threaten me. I will help anyway, in return for…'

'Yes?'

'For information back. About where you are from and how you got here. I'm a light engineer. Your vehicle uses quantum photon jets? Tell me what they are and how they work and I will help you.'

Sorin threw his head back, opened his mouth and a staccato gasping 'ha' sound came from his mouth. 'It's a deal,' he said. 'Now… we need to… discuss things.'

Gant showed Sorin around his house-cube. 'Urinate and defaecate in here,' he said. 'And wash in here. This is the kitchen.'

'It is tiny,' said Sorin. 'Kitchen, living room, bathroom – but where is the…' The translator crackled. Sorin paused. 'Um… Translator failure? Where you… lie down… stop work at… when the sunlight goes and it gets dark.'

Gant looked at him in confusion. How could the sunlight go?

'Light then dark then light, as the sun… moves. You understand?' Sorin said.

'Sun moves?' exclaimed Gant. 'We go round the sun; our planet moves. What do you mean?'

'Oh!' Sorin stood up and stared out of the glass side of Gant's house-cube at the glow of sunlight on the heatside horizon, and round at the other house-cubes with their similar glass sides facing the distant light. 'The sun doesn't set! Their planet doesn't turn… a ribbon of habitable land. A ribbon world. Light on one side, dark on the other.'

Sorin fired questions at Gant, who answered and questioned Sorin in return, until his mouth was dry from talking. 'I will fetch us some more water,' he said. When he came back into the living room from the kitchen, he found Sorin speaking rapidly and incomprehensibly into a square, flickering device on the table. Sorin stopped and, with his strange blue eyes with the black circles in the middle, looked up at Gant.

'Sending information back to my government. It will take… No, I can't translate times accurately! Frustrating!'

'How does your translator know our language?'

'We have been… monitoring your transmission. Our scientists are clever. They worked out common words… 90% accurate, they say.' He walked to the glass side of the house-cube. 'Those,' he said pointing outside, 'are they male or female? I can't tell. You all wear… the same cloaks. And no visible… genitalia.'

Gant looked out and saw several people getting out of a slider and walking along the street towards a large

65

house-cube. 'The taller, stronger ones are female,' he said.

'Strange. On our world it is… the other way around.'

'What — that females are weaker than males?' He paused. 'I thought you were female because of your height.'

Sorin opened his mouth wide, tipped his head back and made the odd, staccato 'ha' sounds again. Gant stared. What was he doing?

'Now, I need to… check my transport's power levels. And that it is still there,' Sorin said. 'That no one… has found it.' He opened some of the cases he had carried, pressed buttons and stared at a small screen.

'That is unlikely. Very few travel darkside. It is too cold, too stormy and too dangerous to venture far there.'

'Doesn't your government… scientists… monitor movements?'

'Why should they?'

Sorin lifted his shoulders and dropped them but said nothing.

'I have been wanting to ask you,' Gant said. 'What is that? The tube on your face?'

'This?' Sorin said, tapping the narrow tube. 'Breathing… It feeds me additional oxygen and… scrubs out the high CO_2 in your atmosphere. And I wanted to ask you something. On your hand… Those wires and meshes…'

'It's my comms glove. Communications. Everyone has one. They are all connected. We use them to send and receive messages, or I can talk into it or tap codes. The lights give information too.'

Sorin reached over and touched the glove on Gant's hand. 'Fascinating…' he murmured.

'Sorin, we have talked enough. I wish to go to work,' Gant said. 'When I'm done, I'll come back.'

Sorin opened his eyes wide and stood up. 'No!' he said. 'I can't risk… I can't trust you to come back. Not to tell…'

'I won't tell. And I will come back.'

'But… I won't know that you'll come back. Or how long… there's no word… No words!' Sorin shouted, striding around the room.

'When I'm done, I'll come back,' Gant said calmly.

'No… I don't think… I can't trust you!'

'You have to. Look,' Gant said, holding out his comms glove, 'I could have tapped out an emergency code at any point. I didn't.'

When Gant returned from work, Sorin was on his back on the floor. His eyes were closed and his mouth was open, showing pale, square teeth. Gant's thick cloak was folded under his head.

'Sorin?' Gant said.

There was no response, except for a long, guttural snort. This must be the 'sleep' that Sorin had talked about. It had been hard to believe that he had come from a distant planet, harder still to accept that his planet turned so that light followed dark and that almost all his planet was habitable. But that his entire species, and animals, stopped work, lay down and went unconscious when the dark came? It was nonsense. But it appeared that it was true.

Gant sat and watched Sorin gasp, grunt and twitch. Suddenly, after a loud shuddering breath, Sorin jerked and shifted, his eyes opened and he lay still, gazing at the ceiling. He said something incomprehensible in a relaxed tone of voice. Then he sat up and tapped his translator button.

'I needed that,' he said, stretching his mouth to show his teeth in a grimace. 'I need food too.'

He went over to his case, took out some things that looked like craen biscuits and ate two.

'Good,' he said. 'Now I feel better. We need to talk more. I need more… information.'

Sorin looked up from the notes he was writing, and watched as Gant worked on a piece of complex equipment, occasionally glancing at the diagrams he had made from Sorin's explanation about the photon jets. After the hours of talking and questioning, Sorin was used to Gant's strange appearance: to his single nostril, his body covered with dark brown fur except for his palms and soles, his stubby fingers and squat build. But he was still fascinated by the alien's dexterity. Gant had two thumbs on each hand – now that would be useful, Sorin thought. Maybe the genetic manipulators back home would be able to engineer that.

Gant put his tools down and pushed the equipment aside. 'I will prepare some food,' he said. 'I am hungry. I assume you will prefer to eat your own food?'

'Yes,' Sorin said. 'I can't risk eating yours.'

As Gant went into the kitchen, Sorin pulled out his transmitter and spoke into it.

'More information. They have no day or night and they do not sleep. There is no word for bed, bedroom, holiday, hours or minutes. They have no seasons. The only time measurements they use are small, for heartbeats, and vast, for the cycle as their planet goes round the sun in a slight elliptical orbit. This appears to be about fifty of our years.'

He paused and glanced at his notebook.

'As far as I can gather, events are triggered not by time or dates but by pressures. For example, Gant works at a water purification plant. He stops work when he needs food or wishes to do something else, not when he has worked a given amount of time. When the plant has sold a certain amount of water then he and his fellow workers are paid a proportion. Similarly, they have democracy, but an election only happens after a given proportion of voters have requested one. It is hard to understand how it works. This may be due to translator problems. I have been here over forty-seven hours…'

He stopped, rubbed his eyes and stretched out his arms. The stronger gravity was grinding him down, despite the muscle-enhancements and circulation-pumps built into his suit. Sleep had helped, but his lungs ached and the joints in his shoulders, legs and arms throbbed.

Gant came back into the living room. He was tapping at the comms glove on his hand.

'Sorin,' he said. 'I have news. It is not good. Your transport…' He paused and looked down at the patterns of lights on the wire meshes on his glove.

'What?'

'Some engineers from the water plant had to go deep darkside to unblock a snowfield pipe. They saw your transport. The government has been informed. My colleague tells me they are planning to fence it off. There are troops, scientists, engineers, officials coming to investigate it.'

'Damn!' Sorin said and stood up. He strode around the living room, then grabbed the case with the link to his transport and switched on the computer. 'It's still shielded. They won't be able to… easily get into it. I don't think they can damage it. But I will need to get to it! Did you say troops? Armed?'

'Probably.'

'How am I going to get back?'

'I do not know.'

Sorin thought hard. It sounded like it would be too dangerous to get back to it.

'Perhaps if I move it…' he said.

'Can you? How?'

'It has remote control and I have a beacon that will call it. But I'm not sure I can… The ship needs more power. It needs light to recharge.'

'But it is in the darkside!' Gant said. 'We are on the darkside'

'I know! I didn't know that this was a… ribbon world!' Sorin thumped the table. 'It was a mistake!'

'How much power does it have left? Can you move it heatside? Into the light?'

'How far is that?'

'To get past the Meridian and its buildings into the remote heatside? We would need to go almost a thousand kilometres, from here, to be far enough away for no one to see it.'

Sorin looked at the dials on the screen and tapped out a few calculations. There was just enough juice left in the ship's energy stores, if he was lucky.

'Maybe. If it doesn't have to go too high. But I'll need to get the beacon there to call it.'

Gant walked around the room, then looked at the steady glow of the pale green sky outside. After a while, he turned to Sorin. 'We would need a heatside slider to go that far. I can get one, but I would have to share the secret with someone.'

Sorin looked up and shook his head. 'No!' he said.

'She, Aiklin, is someone I can trust. She would not tell anyone. We met at University, studying light physics. She works for the energy farms and can give us a heatside slider.'

'I don't like it! How do you know she won't tell anyone?'

'She won't. Whatever we do will be risky. Even this plan. We would have to go through the Meridian suburbs and you… you are different. People might notice.'

A few hours later, having checked the necessary calculations as best he could given the information he had received from Gant, Sorin packed away his computers and communications equipment and doublechecked that the beacon was present and fully-charged in its case.

Gant came in. 'I have arranged to meet Aiklin,' he said, and took a satchel from a hook by the door.

'What is in that?'

'Money, my ID, a water flask, food.'

Sorin opened the lid of one of his cases and took out his spare gun. 'You have guns here too, don't you?' he said.

'Yes. We do, I'm afraid.'

'Machine guns? Rocket guns…?'

'I don't know what you mean. How can a gun be a machine? What are rocket guns?'

'Nothing. Here,' Sorin said, handing it to Gant. 'In case. Can you use it?'

'I think so, but I'm not a soldier,' Gant said.

'Just point and shoot.'

'I'm not sure I can.'

'You may have to. It might be dangerous!'

'Yes. Very well. I will take it,' Gant said. 'Wear this cloak. It has a hood and it joins at the front. It will cover your suit. And you had better wear your helmet and visor. It will look odd—'

'—but not as odd as my face,' Sorin finished Gant's sentence for him.

In the slider, Gant tapped codes into a panel. The joystick folded down and the vehicle moved towards a street of low house-cubes. Sorin stared out of the window at the rectangular fields of ochre, red and dark purple vegetation and the areas of lavender grass scattered with squat lizards. Gant leaned back and closed his eyes. The slider latched onto a rail at a junction, twisted round and sped up. The rails banked steeply upwards on tall pylons to join dozens of other rails, twenty metres above the ground.

Sorin gasped. 'You could have warned me!' he said.

'Warned you about what?'

'It's like a… roller slider… a fun ride… but worse!'

'Roller slider?'

It was worse than the g-force simulator that he'd been flung around on during training, Sorin thought. He tightened his lips against the nausea, gripped the arms of the seat and stared at the swinging and tilting horizon as the rail banked again.

'Don't worry about how slow this is,' Gant said, his eyes still closed. 'We're only on the outer rails. When we join the main cross-Meridian highway we'll go much faster.'

Sorin gripped harder. The slider sped up as it climbed. Soon they were going so fast and so high that Sorin could not make out what was on the ground below them. As other vehicles shot past, Sorin could not help flinching.

'It's better to shut your eyes,' Gant said. 'It's completely safe. It's light-controlled by computers.'

'It doesn't feel safe,' Sorin muttered. Several birds, with wide transparent wings like dragonflies and long thin beaks, fluttered past in the distance. Sorin watched them. 'Don't you have flying?' he said.

'Flying? No. We tried it, but it was too difficult. And the cost was too much. The controlled rails are far safer and fast enough.'

The higher gravity, Sorin thought. That would make powered flight too hard. Ahead were more houses, then complexes of buildings that looked like factories, low dark brown trees like palms and, on the horizon, tower-like buildings interlaced with rails and speeding vehicles. The slider sped towards the low sun.

'How far?' Sorin asked.

'Another eight hundred kilometres.'

'And how long... No, forget it.' Sorin gritted his teeth in frustration. He knew that Gant could not answer. How could a race live without watches and hours and schedules?

When the rails descended into the Meridian centre, they slid heatside through wide buildings. Scooter-type vehicles hovered along the roads, followed by bulky vehicles full of fur-covered people like Gant. Others bustled along pavements and threaded across the roads. Sorin stared around at the glass shop fronts, the flashing video signs and advertisements and the blinking lights that ran along the edges of the roads and pavements.

'It's a bit like London. Before it all,' he said quietly.

'London? What is that?'

'Nothing. But it's so quiet. Where is everyone?' Sorin said as he looked around.

'Everyone? But this is crowded.'

'Tell me, Gant, what is your population? How many people on your world?'

'About 21 million.'

'Is that all? So few… but I suppose only a fraction, a ribbon, is habitable.'

Gant guided the slider into an open archway at the base of a building. Sorin peered through the gloom and saw more lights marking out bays. A car park, he thought, and almost laughed at the banality of it.

As they came out the heat struck Sorin. Twenty-five, thirty degrees, he estimated. Clouds covered the sky overhead, but he glimpsed the pale yellow sun between two buildings. It was just above the horizon, but it still glared brightly against a green sky.

'Yes. We are heatside now,' Gant said. 'This way.'

They turned into an alley. There was a peppery, rank scent of sweat, caramelised sugar and something like burnt onions, as if there was a fast food shop nearby. Sorin could hear voices talking and a syncopated melodic whistle, almost musical but with no obvious rhythm or tune, coming from barred windows above the alley.

'We are better using the back streets and alleys,' Gant said. 'You are conspicuous. If anyone sees you… Pull your visor down and fasten your cloak. The hatcheries are several blocks away.'

'Hatcheries?' Sorin asked. 'I thought you said Aiklin works at the… energy farms?'

'She's at the hatcheries now, helping, because she's laid. I'll help there too, when you're gone. When she wanted to lay, she asked me and I was honoured to give her my sperm.'

Sorin paused and stared at him, but Gant's voice and manner were calm, as if he had merely been talking about lending her a book. Was it a translator error?

A few blocks later they came to a quiet square with blue-leaved shrubs and people sitting on benches facing gravelled paths. Gant walked up to a tall grey building and called Aiklin on his comms glove. A few moments later the door opened. Sorin hadn't fully appreciated how completely different females were from males. Aiklin had rich tawny fur, long arms and legs, wide eyes with a vertical pupil within a striated gold-brown iris and a broad face with marked cheekbones. Like Gant, she had the meshes and lights of a comms glove on one hand.

'Gant,' she said. 'Greetings.'

Gant touched foreheads with her. She examined Sorin, looking him up and down, her head on one side. He pushed his visor up and she gasped and turned to Gant.

'Yes,' he said. 'This is Sorin. As I said, from another world.'

'So it's true!' Aiklin said.

'True. I'll tell you more afterwards, but we need to get this heatside slider.'

'Wait,' said Sorin, putting his visor back down. 'Can I… I would like to see the hatcheries. I need more… information.'

'Can we?' Gant asked Aiklin.

75

'Yes, if we are careful. There are not many others here at the moment, but we must keep this visit secret. I'll take you to the quieter hatchery.'

She led them along a corridor to a low-ceilinged, cool and windowless room. In wide trays filled with blue straw-like bedding, under shining lamps, were hundreds of blotched purple and dark-red eggs, each as large as Sorin's head. Some were rocking gently. There were a dozen other fur-covered people strolling through the room, looking at the eggs, reading dials on screens or consulting papers in their hands. Sorin pulled his hood further over his head, but they only glanced curiously at him, Aiklin and Gant, then moved on.

'This is only one of the eight hatcheries here,' said Aiklin. 'It is a small one. Only five hundred eggs. The nurseries are in the floors above us.'

'Is one yours?' Sorin asked her.

She tipped her head and gazed at him, then turned to Gant. 'Mine?' she said.

'You and Gant – are some of the eggs yours? How do you know which ones are yours?'

'Does it matter?' said Gant.

'But…'

Suddenly Sorin understood why the house-cubes were so small and why the translator failed with words like family, child, father, love. He turned away and gazed at the expanse of unmarked restless eggs. He remembered his five-year old son. He had died from radiation poisoning, six months after his mother.

He blinked hard and turned back to Gant. 'We should go. I've seen enough,' he said.

When they came to the entrance, Aiklin gave Gant a small silver orb.

'It's in the storage seven blocks heatside from here. You know the one. Bring it back unmarked!' she said.

'I will,' Gant said. 'I'll come back here, and then we can talk. You need to learn what Sorin has told me. Especially about his technology. Aiklin, the things we could do with it!'

'Yes! You must tell me!' she said, then turned to Sorin. 'I hope all goes well for you.'

They made their way on towards the block where Aiklin's slider was through a series of narrow streets, but as they went along a deserted alley Sorin heard someone running towards them. Suddenly, he was seized from behind. A knife slid against his throat.

'Don't move,' a voice hissed. 'Got money?'

Sorin shook his helmeted head and called out to Gant, 'Don't be a hero!' He was relieved to see that Gant stood, watching, and wasn't going to move. Sorin shifted his feet slightly. He knew what to do. They'd done enough of this in training. He stepped rapidly back and slammed the mugger against the alley wall, then grabbed his arm and rolled him forward and over his shoulder until he crashed onto his back on the ground.

Gant fumbled in his bag and pulled out the gun. Sorin could see that his fingers were too big to fit into the trigger. The figure on the ground struggled to his feet and launched himself at Sorin. Gant waved the gun. There was a brief flash of light. The knifeman yelled and fell to his knees. Dark brown blood seeped from his back and stained his fur.

'Run!' Sorin yelled.

They ran round the corner and down another two alleys, then into a broader street.

'I think we're far enough away,' Sorin said, pausing. 'Which way is the slider park now?'

'That way. Perhaps we should have kept to the main streets,' Gant panted.

Gant's heart didn't seem to want to stop thumping in his chest. He'd never even fired a gun before, let alone hurt someone. He thought of the blood spreading on the ground and the mugger writhing in pain. For an instant he thought of stopping and calling for help on his comms glove, but he couldn't risk the complications and explanations.

As they entered the slider park, Sorin slowed and staggered.

'Did he hurt you?' Gant asked.

'No… I'm alright. I just need to rest…' Sorin said. 'Get the slider…'

Gant clicked the metal orb. A large white slider inched forward from a recess. Its doors opened. Sorin collapsed onto the seat inside, his head back, his eyes closed. He was gasping for breath.

Gant shoved the orb into its holder and started the slider. He flipped the coolant system to max, moved out and headed through the blocks and suburbs towards the sun. As the last few house-cubes receded behind them he sped up. On the left were row upon row of gantries holding thousands of photovoltaic squares gazing towards the dazzling sun. Sorin lifted his head to look at them.

'Energy farms?' Sorin whispered.

'Yes.'

'Do you have… nuclear energy?'

'No. What is that?'

'Nothing,' he muttered and his head flopped backwards again.

The light grew brighter as they raced onwards, clouds of red and orange dust blooming behind them. Gant twisted the dial to darken the windscreen. They were at least five hundred kilometres from the Meridian, and the energy farms were far behind them.

'Sorin?' he said. 'How far do we need to go?'

Sorin stirred and mumbled something unintelligible.

'How far?' Gant repeated. Despite the coolant, the temperature in the slider was climbing to thirty degrees, and outside it had hit fifty. The smell of hot oil filled the slider. Gant didn't dare go much further. It could reach several hundred degrees in the vast plains heatside. He stopped the slider.

Sorin was gasping for breath. His over-thick lips were no longer pink but turning white. He tipped forward, his head between his knees. Then Gant saw it. The knife had snagged the tube and pulled it away from Sorin's suit. The tube had a ragged split in it.

Gant shook Sorin.

'Your air supply! The oxygen tube – it's cut!' he shouted.

'That's… not good…' Sorin muttered.

'Is there another? A spare tube? Something! You must have something to fix it!'

Sorin slumped further. Gant wrenched open the locker by his feet, then twisted round to check the back. There must be a medical kit – yes, there on the shelf. He grabbed it and tipped the contents out. No oxygen flasks, but he found bandages, pins – tape! As fast as he could, he cut strips of tape and wound them around the tube, trying to seal the crack without compressing the oxygen

79

flow. The tape was porous, but if he wrapped enough layers round... Sweat slicked his palms and dripped through the fur on his forehead.

Sorin lifted his head. His eyes opened. He breathed in and shuddered.

'What happened? My head... dizzy...'

'Keep still. I think the oxygen is coming through now. Wait. I'll get the beacon. Can you set it?'

'Yes, I think so,' he said, and paused. He put his head down for a moment, then lifted it and breathed deeply. 'Hand it to me. How far have we come?'

'About five hundred kilometres from the Meridan.'

'It should be enough.' He fiddled with the dials and touchpads on the beacon and handed it to Gant. His breathing was noisy and laboured. 'There – it's on,' he panted. 'Put it out. Then move back.'

Gant got a heatside cloak from the locker, wrapped it around himself then switched on its cooling system. The white cloth around his head and shoulders flexed as the coolant flowed through the microfibres. He stepped out into the heat and dazzling glare. He gasped despite the cooling cloak. The heatside wind scorched his throat. Even with the cloaks, they would not survive in this oven. The sky overhead was a polished vibrant green and the air on the horizon shimmered. Gant shaded his eyes and looked around, but he could see nothing except ochre sand and rocks and flatness and heavy stacks of emerald clouds over the Meridian. He placed the beacon and reeled back to the slider.

A red light on the beacon flashed as they waited.

'Fingers crossed,' muttered Sorin.

'What?' The phrase was lost in translation.

'Just hope…'

The red light turned orange. Then a flickering green light appeared.

'Good. It's on its way,' mumbled Sorin.

'Are you recovered?'

'No. Still not getting enough…'

Gant heard a steady hum that grew to a vibrating roar before he saw the huge grey vehicle in the sky above. The sand billowed around it as it descended. The photon jets were silent and dark. It seemed, as far as Gant could tell, to be using a hover function like the sliders did.

It settled a few metres away from the beacon. A ramp dropped open.

'At last,' croaked Sorin. 'I need oxygen. Gant, I don't think I can stand up. Too weak…'

Gant fastened another cloak around Sorin and lifted him. Despite his thinness, he was heavy. Gant wished he was as strong as Aiklin. The weight pulled his arms and back, and every gasping breath was a fire in his mouth. In the shadow of the ovoid it was marginally easier. He gathered himself, heaved Sorin over his shoulders and stumbled up the ramp.

It was cooler inside. Sorin whispered, 'Close doors,' and they sealed shut behind them. Gant sank to his knees and Sorin slid facedown to the floor. 'Oxygen… water…' he muttered.

Gant looked around desperately. He could see control desks, a chair, lockers, a large imager panel on a wall, doors, screens and switches – all labelled in unreadable symbols. Where would water and oxygen be? He opened a drawer at random, then another. He heard a click behind him. Turning round, he saw a small cylinder on wheels, with blinking sensors and robotic claws, holding a tube and what was – yes, must be – a gas mask. It rolled over to Sorin and placed them by his side. He clawed sideways to reach them, rammed the mask over his face and rolled onto his back. The robot whirred off and returned with a beaker. Water, Gant assumed. He flipped the lid open, drank half and gave the rest to Sorin.

'I'll get your cases,' he said. Pulling the cloak around himself, he went back out into the scorching heat.

By the time he'd brought everything in, his legs and arms were shaking, and his fur drenched and dark with sweat. Sorin seemed to have recovered. He had apparently changed his suit for another with a working tank and tube and sat at a control panel, flicking switches and watching dials.

'It will be fully charged soon. This light... so bright. No problems,' he said.

Gant watched him for a while, then went towards him. He touched his shoulder.

'Sorin? I think I had better go,' he said. He was surprised how sad he felt.

Sorin stood too. He had an odd expression on his face, one Gant had never seen before. Sorin strode to and fro, shook his head a few times, then turned to face Gant.

'Come with me,' he said.

'What?'

'Come with me. You are curious, I know. To see what my planet is like.'

Gant froze for a heartbeat. To go with Sorin? To see a world that turned. To experience light then dark, to see stars in a cloud-free night sky, to learn what they knew of technology, physics, light... and never return? He thought of Aiklin and what she would do. She would go. She was braver than him.

'No,' he said, with regret. 'I cannot. This is my home. I have promised to tell Aiklin and others about what you have taught me. We can develop our technology using yours. I should stay.'

Sorin raised and dropped his shoulders, then turned away. He pulled something out of a locker and stood, with his back to Gant, looking down at it. He sighed.

'Sorin?' said Gant. 'I will leave. Goodbye, my friend.'

Sorin turned. In his hand was a syringe. He darted forward and wrenched the comms glove off Gant's hand. Before Gant could react, Sorin rammed the needle into his shoulder. Something – a fizzing, stinging liquid – spread through his blood. The drug leached strength from him. His muscles gave way and he collapsed.

Sorin knelt next to him.

'What…' Gant stuttered. The drug was clamping his mouth.

'You have to come,' said Sorin. 'I have to take back a… specimen. My orders.'

Gant tried to get up and throw himself on Sorin. But his limbs refused him.

'It's a paralyser,' Sorin said. 'Then I'll put you into suspension. They want… Gant, they need a living specimen.'

He crouched close to Gant. I saved your life, Gant wanted to shout, but he could not move his tongue. Sorin's mouth was twisted. Water was trickling from his eyes and running down his face. His words were fading. Gant couldn't see any more, then, like the clouds darkside, cold blackness spread through him.

Sound came back. Gant could hear humming motors and quiet mechanical clicks, but he could see nothing. He felt something cold and hard on his wrist. It was a metal manacle attached to a chain. He fumbled along the chain. It was attached to another manacle locked to a rail on the control desk. The black fog thinned. He looked round. The ramp was wide open, light shone in, and he could see sand drifting in the hot desert wind outside. They hadn't moved. He was still home. Gant wrenched at the manacle.

Sorin came up the ramp. When his eyes met Gant's fury, he pulled out his gun and aimed it at Gant. Gant lunged at him.

'Calm down,' Sorin said. 'I need to tell you something.'

Gant roared back. 'You bastard! I trusted you!'

'No. Calm down! I'm going to… to rescue you!'

'Liar!' yelled Gant.

'Yes! Liar! Gant, you have to get to the slider. I'm going to unlock this and walk you outside. To the slider. You have to see something, then I'll let you go. Can you stand?'

Gant stood up and tried to lunge at Sorin, but his legs shook. He could barely walk. He couldn't fight, he realised. He couldn't even run. He was helpless. Keeping the gun trained on him, Sorin unlocked the manacle and threw the other cloak around him.

'Put it on, switch it on. Don't run. If you do, I'll shoot,' he said. 'Go on. Out.'

Gant stumbled down the ramp to the slider. Sorin pushed him inside. Gant tried to resist, but Sorin snapped, 'Don't make this difficult!' and manacled his wrist to the door handle, then he went back in and came out with several cases, which he pushed into the back of the slider. Beads of water had appeared on his face. 'The heat…' he muttered. He put a smaller metal rectangle, along with several rolls of paper, into Gant's lap. 'Computer,' he said. 'And maintenance plans and information. For the photon jets. Must rest…'

He leaned against the slider, in the shade, and stood there, panting and wiping his face. Gant stared at him, puzzled. Then Sorin stumbled back and returned with more crates and cases. He had a large grey tube slung round his shoulders. There was an odd, restless excitement in his manner. He turned, clicked a device in his hand and the ramp lifted and closed, then he got into the slider, pulled out a beaker and drank. Then he passed it to Gant. 'There. Drink. I'm done. Tough… so hot out there,' he said. 'But I'm done. Move the slider back. About a kilometre.'

'Why? Why should I do anything you ask?' Gant shouted.

'Just do it! Do it!' Sorin yelled back, pointing the gun at him.

Gant stared at him with bewilderment. Nothing seemed to make sense. Slowly, he started the slider and moved it backwards until Sorin said, 'Stop!'

Sorin got out and took the grey tube from his shoulders. He stood by the slider with his feet wide apart. The heatside wind blew his cloak aside. He breathed in deeply, shifted his feet and aimed the tube towards his transport. Gant started, his heart beating fast. There was an ear-splitting sound, like gunfire from a thousand guns, and yellow-orange flares blazed and rippled on the outside of the ovoid. Tiny cracks bloomed on its surface. Sorin fired again and again and again.

'Shield should be down now,' Sorin muttered.

He adjusted something on the tube and fired again. The ovoid shattered with a roar that cracked pain through

Gant's eardrums. He put his hands over his ears and stared in horror as huge fragments of metal and glass fountained upwards. Sorin threw himself into the slider and slammed the door shut as shards and debris poured down onto it. The sound of the explosion and the falling debris rolled around them.

Sorin leaned back and closed his eyes. 'I couldn't do it,' he said after a while. 'I couldn't...'

'Do what? What is going on?'

'Gant, we sent out nine transports. Like mine. To research... spy out possible planets. This planet, your people, Gant, it's ideal...'

'Ideal for what?'

'You have no nuclear weapons, no machine guns. There's not many of you. You don't even have flying transports. You're almost primitive.'

'Primitive! Us?'

'Yes. It would be easy.'

'Easy for what, Sorin?'

'You remember I said trade? No. That was a lie. Not trade. The plan is to—' Sorin cut himself short. He put his head into his hands and was silent. Then he looked directly at Gant, his blue eyes wide open and his mouth thin. 'Gant, the plan is to invade.'

'Invade! What do you mean – invade?'

'We had no choice. Nuclear war. There is barely anything left. But I couldn't do it...'

'Sorin, you are making no sense. Couldn't do what?'

'Let you be invaded. Let you die. I think it will work. I sent them a transmission telling them you had nuclear weapons, that you were aggressive, violent, numerous, armed...'

Gant closed his eyes as the realisation hit him like a blast of heatside air. An invasion… His heart raced and the fur on his head and chest rose as fear drenched him.

'Invasion… I don't understand,' he muttered. He looked around at the turmoil of ripped cloth and paper and plastic shards swirling around the slider. 'But – you fired on your transport. You destroyed it!'

'Yes. It has comms with the government. At the first shots it will send messages saying that it is under fire. Then when they realise the shield was breached and there's nothing more, I hope… I hope they'll be warned off. If not, you can prepare. I can help. I can show you our technology.'

Gant breathed in, out, in again. His raised fur settled as he understood. 'But… but what about you? You'll never be able to get back!' he said.

'I have nothing left there,' Sorin said quietly, looking at the sun on the distant horizon. 'Nothing. No one. All dead… That is why I volunteered.'

Water glistened in his eyes and trickled down his furless cheeks. He rubbed his eyes and dropped his head. Then he turned to Gant.

'We'd better move before someone notices or tracks us,' he said. 'But first…'

He threw the gun out of the window. He looked at the metal and crystalline rectangle on his wrist that, as he had told Gant, measured time. He undid it and flung it out too. He leaned over and unlocked the manacle on Gant's wrist.

'Now… we are both free,' he said.

FIRST CONTACT

Tegon Maus

"Are you sure?" she asked staring at the floor.

"Yes, very," I returned.

"I think…" she began, cupping her hand over her mouth for a moment, "I think it's important that you understand this is an all or nothing situation."

"I do. I understand completely. I told you… I'm OK with it."

"It's my fault… I just…"

"Doc, look, I get it, there's no room for failure. I won't let you down. You'll see."

"I'm just not sure if you're ready, that's all," she said softly, turning her back to me.

"Are you kidding me? I've been a marine for more than twenty years. I'm the top in my field. I've had the best training available. I've been on dozens of assignments far more critical than this and I came out on top every time. You have to trust me… I can handle it."

"A marine for twenty years? The best training? I'm not sure that will be enough to guarantee your success," she said with a soft smile.

"Well, it will have to do," I said confidently.

"I guess it will. I would feel better if you had a safe word," she offered lightly.

"A safe word? For what?" I was beginning to feel like she didn't trust me or my abilities.

"In case you need backup."

"Backup? Really?"

"There's no shame in asking for a little help in a tough spot. A good marine would ask for backup," she prodded.

"A good marine is all the backup anyone would need," I returned proudly.

"Alright, have it your way. You'll have three hours... no more... no less. We begin in 15," she said stiffly.

"I'm ready."

"Give'm hell, marine," she said over her shoulder as she turned to leave.

I watched her until she was out of sight. Only then did my true feelings come to the surface. I had misgivings... concerns that I dare not share with her. If she saw any weakness, any hesitation in me, even the slightest, all bets would be off and I couldn't live with that. No matter how I felt about it, I had to pull this off... no matter what.

The sound of a door sliding open at the end of the causeway drew my attention.

"Ahh, shit. Here we go," I said under my breath.

Walking straight toward me, dressed in a pink T-shirt, blue jeans and barefoot, was the Doc's seven-year-old daughter. Her dark hair was pulled back into a ponytail and tied with a thin, pink ribbon. She was her mother's daughter alright. I could see the Doc's cheek bones and the shape of her nose from here.

"Hello... Sam?" I called cheerfully.

Nothing... no answer, no smile, no reaction at all.

"Damn it," I whispered. This was going to be tougher than I thought. "Hello," I said for a second time, stepping closer.

"Are we there yet?"

"I'm sorry. What did you say?"

"Are we there yet? It's a simple question. Mother said we were almost there. I'm awake now and she sent me here to see you... are we there yet?"

"No. Not just yet. It will be a day or two longer. By the way, I'm Robert Wickham... my friends call me Bob," I said offering my hand.

"You know she's smarter than you," she said with disinterest, refusing to shake my hand.

"Beg your pardon?"

"My mother. She's way smarter than you," she repeated. This time her voice held a little arrogance in it.

"Yeah, I think so as well," I said honestly.

"Actually she's way smarter than almost everyone," she bragged.

"Yeah, I think you might be right with that one," I agreed, hoping to find common ground.

"Oh, I am. Mother has an IQ of 135... the average is 94, so she's much smarter than almost everyone."

"Good to know," I returned, not sure where we were going with this.

"Mine is 183," she boasted.

"Your what?" I asked, trying to divide my attention between her and the bank of dials and monitors.

"My IQ... it's 183. Einstein's was 164," she said pointedly.

"You don't say... Einstein. Well, how about that? Your mom said you were a smart little girl," I heard myself say. I was lost. I had no idea what to say next.

"Do you love her?" she asked suddenly, pushing to stand in front of me, separating me from the panel.

"What?" I gasped, moving backward a little.

"I said… do you love her?" she asked again, stepping to stand in front of me again. "Are you hard of hearing or are you just slow?"

"It's complicated," I answered before thinking.

"That's not an answer," she scolded, folding her arms, stepping closer still.

"I don't think you would understand. It's an adult thing," I said trying to regain some authority, stepping back again.

"I'm seven, not stupid, and I have an IQ of 183. I think I can handle it," she sneered stepping closer, trying to stare me down.

My mind raced, searching for an out. I had to take control.

"Okay. This isn't going to plan. Let's start over as equals… 100% honest with each other… no holds barred. Agreed?" I offered my hand, stepping forward.

"Agreed," she said taking my hand.

"Robert Wickham… call me Bob."

"Samantha Fremont… call me Sam."

"Good. Glad to meet you, Sam. So then, you first, ask what you want," I said folding my arms.

"Did she give you a safe word?"

"No, but she wanted to."

"Are you planning to marry my mom?"

"Yes, that's the plan… contingent on your approval. You OK with that?"

"I'll have to think about it."

"I love your mom… I'm not looking to take your dad's place."

"I have no dad… sperm donor."

"I see."

"How did you meet?"

"Here on the job. She's medical… I'm transport."

"What do you do in transport?"

"I'm a sector chief. I'm responsible for more than 100,000 pods."

"That didn't tell me what you do."

This was going to be tough. She wasn't going to cut me any slack.

"See these dials and monitors? They maintain the pods and where each should go. This ship holds a little over two million pods."

"Pods?"

"Ahh sorry. Each pod holds one person… each held in stasis… suspended animation, as it were, to be able to handle the long trip here. The ship starts out from Earth orbit and makes a stop about every six months, refuels and picks up a new crew. Twelve crews and six years later they arrive here. My crew and I sort them by occupation and destination and help to send them on their way."

"And my mom?"

"She usually rides the last leg… one or two weeks out before turning around. Our jobs cross… we met and fell in love."

"Why am I here?"

"To meet me and…"

"And?"

"I have a couple of acres down on the planet. I'm looking to retire and I've asked your mom to start a new life with me there."

"I've never been on a real planet before."

"I know… your mom talks about it all the time. I think you'll like it."

"You think so?"

"I do. My place has lots of grass… a couple of horses, some ducks and even a chicken or two."

"I've never seen a real horse either."

"You'll like them. They're fun to ride."

Silence… she just stood there.

Damn it. I screwed up. I said something wrong… I've lost her. The thought burned hot in my head.

"Everything OK?" I asked.

She only nodded in response.

"Let me ask one. Why are you barefoot?"

"I like the way the cold metal feels on the bottom of my feet."

"Yeah, I know what you mean. You got one more for me?"

"Sure… are we there yet?"

WHEN FRIDAY NEVER COMES

Devon Rosenblatt

Monday

Today is the first day back from the holidays and I cannot wait to see all my friends again.

I enjoy learning and I cannot wait until second period when we will start a new topic on the history syllabus – modern history. History is my favourite subject, learning about how people used to live and how things have changed over time.

There have been a lot of changes in recent decades, in robotics above all other areas. Twenty years ago there were no sentient automatons to be seen on the street.

On school days I get picked up from the shelter at around 08:00 and arrive at school for 08:45. I use this time to say hello to my friends Scarlet, Eve and Rex and catch up with all that has happened over the school break.

As I head to class, I see a kid who I have not seen before. He is dressed like everyone else in a smart blazer, trousers, shirt and tie. His hair is neatly combed too, but he stands out from the rest. He walks ever so funny, somewhat clumsy, and the expressions on his face are very odd.

I think he might be one of them.

I heard they were going to put the new models in different schools to the old in case they would not get along.

In the morning we have registration and assembly followed by the first period. Today we have art first. I do not like art as much as other subjects. I find that the lack of rules and method make it difficult to learn. I do not really get it. Dad says it is outdated and it will not lead to a proper job, but it is an easy grade to get and add towards the total yearly score to graduate. 'You can make up any nonsense and get a pass,' Dad says.

The new kid is in art class. He is showing the teacher what he has drawn on his electronic sketchpad. He makes the strangest faces as he talks. However, it seems he is really good at art, or so the teacher says as she uploads his work for everyone to see. There are lots of squiggly lines and colours. I do not get what it is supposed to be, but the teacher says it is a 'good example'.

At 10:30 we have our break. All the kids are playing together except for the new kid. He just sits on a bench staring from the corner of the playground. I go to my friend Rex and ask him if he has spoken to the new kid. Rex says he has not but Eve has and that she said he is very weird and must be one of them.

The second period is the part of the day I have been waiting for, modern history. We all sit at our desks and teacher downloads the lesson. My notes say we learn about 'the rise of sentient automatons', 'the AI revolution of the 2030s' and how 'by 2038 most of the human workforce had been replaced by machines.' Those were the notes I made anyway.

The teacher explains this is why many people live in the slums now except for the very rich. The rich could not be replaced she says.

After second period it is time for lunch. All the kids flood the hall. When everyone has refuelled, the hall empties and the playground fills. That is when I notice the new kid again. He had not been present during history and over the first part of lunch, so I had completely forgotten about him. I stare at him only for a short time, but he is quick to see me and starts to come over. Not being sure what to do, I stay where I am.

He stops near me and begins to speak, making the most unusual faces as he does. 'Hello, my name's Max. What's yours?'

'Hi, I am David,' I reply.

'Hi David, will you be my friend?'

'OK,' I say. I am not sure if I really want to be his friend, but it would be bad manners to say no.

He says nothing.

'What do you want to do?' I ask.

'I'm not sure. We could play hide and seek?'

'Sure.' Again, I do not really want to play this game but I cannot think of a reason not to.

'You hide and I'll seek,' he says.

I know about hide and seek but have not played it before – it is a very old game. The rules seem simple enough. Max turns around and starts to count while I look for somewhere to hide. There are not many places as the area is very open – there is behind the sports hut, round the corner to the side of the school or the big tree at the far end of the field. I am still deciding by the time Max reaches 'ten', so I run for the nearest place, behind the sports hut. Max peaks behind the sports hut and sees me standing there.

'Found you! Now it's your turn.'

Before I can say anything, the buzzer goes.

'That's a shame,' Max says. 'Maybe we can play again tomorrow?'

'Maybe,' I reply.

'I know,' he says while making a funny face again along with a strange hand gesture, 'You could come to mine and we could play there.'

'I would have to ask my parents.'

'OK, I'll ask mine too and you could come over Friday after school.'

I agree and we both walk back to the classroom. I am not sure if I want to go over to his house as he is very odd, but I was not sure what else to say. Most likely my parents will not let me anyway.

It is the last period after lunch. We have maths and that goes very quick. I completely forget about Max's invite until later that evening.

Each week Mom takes me with her to the vendors to do the shopping. We both go inside a booth and, once the door closes, there is a flash of light and we are taken into a shopping environment. In the olden days, they did not have these simulations and people would have to spend hours and hours walking up and down lanes to find what they were after. I imagine it used to make everyone very tired and cranky.

It was while Mom was looking at the different choices of oil available that she asks me about my day at school. I tell her about all the interesting stuff I learnt in history and the strange new kid in my class. I do not tell her that he invited me over in case she says yes, but she suggests that he comes over to ours anyway. I say that I do not think he will want to, but she insists. 'Don't be silly, I am sure he will appreciate making a new friend,' she says.

Tuesday

The next day at school starts like the last: I arrive at 08:45, say hello to my friends and chat until the buzzer goes at 09:00. After registration and assembly, we have geography and electronics. Max is at the first but not the second. At lunch, I ask him why he does not have the same classes as me. He says that he was told that some of the classes are 'not relevant' to him and he is to take other ones instead. He did not want to talk too much about it.

He then asks if I want to play another old game. Someone is chosen to be called 'it' and then they must chase and catch the other players. If the person who is the 'it' catches another player, then the one they catch is called 'it' instead. I wonder where he gets all these weird ideas for games from.

Out of nowhere, Max taps me on the shoulder and shouts, 'You're it!' before running off. I think this is where I am supposed to run after him. He runs to the far side of the field, so I do the same. He is very good at this game. Not only is he very quick, but he seems to know which direction I am coming from without looking. It is like he has a tracker. He cannot be one of them if he has a tracker.

I like the game more than I thought I would. I become so engaged that time soon passes and then the buzzer sounds. I am starting to enjoy spending time with Max and I ask him whether he would like to come over to my house the following night. He agrees and makes a face while flapping his arms about in an unusual fashion. He seems to do this when he likes the idea of something. I think I am beginning to understand his behaviour a bit better.

When I return home that evening I tell mum that Max said yes to staying the night, but she says, 'Sorry, it will no longer be possible.' She found out from the head teacher that Max is one of them and says that, 'We do not have the means to accommodate his needs.' I do not like Mom's answer, but she says, 'I will not listen to any more on the subject.'

I go to the other room to speak to Dad.

Dad has downloaded the news and is busy going through the events of the day. I can never get his attention when he is going through the news, so I decide to tune into the programme too. There is a reporter standing in the middle of a street with people running all about the place. The people are pulling faces and making funny gestures – like humans do – but these gestures are very different to the ones I saw Max do when he liked something. Writing scrolls across the bottom of the screen, 'First human protest since 2038'. The whole street appears to be in chaos, with humans breaking stuff and shouting.

Dad says that they never learn and that, 'Such actions do not serve any purpose, yet still they continue with their reckless conduct.'

Wednesday

I arrive at school at 08:45. I look for Max to tell him the bad news about coming to my house, but he is nowhere to be found. I ask my other friends if they know where he is, but they have not seen him.

At 09:00 the buzzer goes and we all head into the hall for registration and assembly. The register is taken and announcements given but, instead of going to first period, we are told to wait where we are. I talk to my friends and no one knows what is going on. The teachers are not saying anything either. I am starting to get a feeling that I have never had before.

I decide to go to the small library in the corner of the hall where they preserve a small collection of physical books. Something in the science section catches my eye. It is a thin, colourful paperback. It is called *Visions of the Future* and on the cover it says it cost '2.50' – I think that was a lot of money back when this book was made.

It is obviously very old and I handle it with care. Inside, there are badly printed pictures and short blocks of text in boxes and squashed circles. One page tells the story of a man who travels across space and dimensions to save the universe with his chainsaw sword. Another page has a list of short sentences titled, 'Fascinating Future Facts'. Another page is headed 'New Emerging Technology – Human Augmentation'.

Man has always sought to enhance his body using inanimate objects ever since early homo-sapiens invented tools. In recent years, it has simply become more advanced with the advent of optics, acoustics, prosthetics and - most recently - artificial intelligence. All have played their part in the betterment of the human form. This pursuit for physical and mental improvement has driven the course of technology to new frontiers.

Technology will continue to be a force for good. It is highly probable that in the future humans will be able to upgrade or replace any body part with a cybernetic equivalent. It is theorised that brain implants will allow for higher levels of cognitive thinking than can currently be imagined…

The book makes a good read and I am so hooked that I almost do not notice the quiet tap on the window. I look across but there is nothing to be seen. I look around to see if anyone else heard the tap, but they are all standing towards the front of the hall. I go over to the window to get a better look. Looking down, I see Max standing below me. His facial expressions are stranger and quicker than ever. I look around to make sure no one is looking and then open the window slightly.

I whisper, 'What are you doing out there?'

'Quick, we need to get out of here!'

'Why?'

'I'll explain on the way, but we need to go now!'

'But I will get in trouble.'

'Please trust me, David. It's not safe here.'

I am not sure what to do. I feel that I should go with him, but I cannot say why. I look around the hall again to make sure no one has seen us talking and carefully push the window open a little bit more. I climb onto the ledge and lower myself down.

Straight away, Max grabs me by the arm and pulls. 'We need to go now!'

I resist. 'Not until you tell me what is going on.'

Max is about to say something but stops at the sound of a distant yelling. We look down the street and see a big group of people heading our way.

Max pulls on my arm again. 'Quick, into this alley.' He drags me across the street before letting go and running down the alley. I stand still, staring at the oncoming crowd. I do not know what to do. I do not want to get into trouble and it may not be too late to go back. I do not understand what it is about the crowd that I should be concerned about.

Max calls to me, but I do not move. I just continue to stare.

The crowd are very close now and I can hear their voices shouting, 'Eradicate the robots,' and 'Annihilate the automatons.'

They are all shouting. They want to destroy us? But why?

Max runs up to my side. 'Why aren't you running?'

'Why would I need to?'

'They're going to kill you.'

'But why would they want to kill me? I do not mean them any harm. It makes no sense.'

'They're angry and things don't need to make sense to people when they're angry.'

The crowd is close. I can clearly see their faces. Their brows are scrunched up and the corners of their lips pulled downwards, just like the expressions of the people in the news report. I do not know what it means, but the feeling it gives me is not one I like. Why are they doing this? How will it help? None of it makes sense.

A man towards the front stops and points in our direction, shouting, 'There's some trying to escape.' He starts to run and then, one at a time, the other humans copy his actions until they are all chasing the first.

'What are they doing now?' I ask.

Max ignores my question and changes the subject. 'David, we're going to play a game.'

'But it is not break or lunch.'

'It doesn't matter,' he says with a strange tone in his voice. 'We're going to play tag.'

'Everything you humans do makes no sense.'

He ignores me again and goes on about his stupid game instead. 'You're going to be "it" first, OK?'

'Why?'

'Why not?' He touches me on the arm and runs shouting, 'Tag, you're it.'

Before I can think about it I run after him, through the alley and out into the street on the other side. Max is getting further away with each stride. He is running faster than he usually does when we play this game. He must really want to win. As he gets even further away, I hear the sound of footsteps behind me. They sound close, but I dare not look back in case it slows me down. I can tell from the noise and the signals on my built-in tracker that there is a large crowd following us. A lot of people must want to play too. I do not understand the humans' obsession with this game.

We run down more alleyways, through a park and across another couple of streets before Max starts to slow down. I can no longer hear the humans' footsteps. I guess they do not want to play anymore. Max stops at a wire fence.

I run up to him. 'Tag, you are it.' And then I begin to run away.

Rather than chase me, Max just stands by the fence and calls out, 'That's the end of the game. You win.'

I stop and turn to face him. 'Do you not want a go?'

'Maybe another day,' he says with the corners of his mouth pulled up. 'Now we need to get into here and play another game.' He pulls at part of the fence where it has come away from the post and squeezes through the gap. 'Follow me.'

We walk through long grass towards a large modern building. Max is walking very slowly and quietly. Again, I am not sure why. Humans seem to do a lot of strange things that make no sense.

Once at the wall of the building, we follow it round until we reach an airduct next to a closed shutter door. Max takes the grating from the airduct and starts to go through on his hands and knees. 'This way!'

I crouch down and begin to follow.

'Don't forget to put the grate back,' he calls back to me before turning a corner.

We crawl for about five minutes, taking one corner after another until we reach an opening blocked by another grate. Max carefully moves it to one side and pokes his head out. He looks around and then crawls out of the ducting into the room beyond. I follow him and am about to speak when he again starts with the funny gestures – this time putting a finger to his mouth.

'What does that mean?' I ask.

He whispers back in that tone of voice he has started using lately, 'Be quiet.'

I think he is trying to answer my question, but I cannot be sure. It would not be the first time he has said something that does not follow on from what we had last been talking about.

I look around the room. It is very large with lots of crates stacked on shelves that reach all the way to the ceiling. Max creeps over to one stack of crates near a conveyer belt. Above it in big red writing it reads 'Loading Bay'.

Max puts his hand on my shoulder and whispers into my ear, 'Now we are going to play hide and seek.'

'Who is hiding?' I ask.

'We both are, and the men in uniforms are seeking. Hide in this crate until I come and get you.'

I climb into the crate and Max shuts the lid.

A long time passes. It seems like hours. At one point, I feel the crate being lifted into the air, swaying from side to side, and then traveling along.

It is like this – with lots and lots of movement – for some time until it finally comes to a rest. Then I wait, and wait, and wait.

Thursday

After recharging, I wake to find myself still inside the crate. It feels like the crate is moving again, but it is neither being lifted nor travelling along. It feels like it is drifting. I listen carefully to the outside sounds. All I can hear is an occasional beep and a low rumble that comes from all directions.

After some time, I finally hear a knock on the side of the crate.

'David, are you there?' It sounds like Max.

'Yes I am,' I reply.

There is no answer, just some more noises – a rattle, some more knocking. Suddenly, light fills the crate and I see Max. I think he is smiling.

'Sorry I took so long. It was hard to find my way here without anyone seeing me.'

I stand up and climb out of the crate. We are in a small round metal room filled with yet more crates. 'Where are we?'

'We're on a spaceship called the *Phoenix*.'

I respond in a tone that I am not used to. 'A spaceship?!' I think I am starting to pick up some human habits.

Max takes me to a small round window on the wall of the room. I peer through and see a black backdrop with small lights scattered across it that span as far as I can see in all directions. Just in front of the backdrop is a large blue and green circle wrapped in a white mist.

Beyond Thursday

Gradually I begin to learn more. Max explained to me that the humans on Earth had started to attack robots on a mass scale. They blamed us for them losing their jobs and not being able to 'contribute towards society' like they used to. Things had quickly got worse until war between humans and robots was a reality. A lot of the rich people, some of whom were augmented, boarded spaceships to escape the war. 'Earth is beyond help,' Max was told, and Max was one of the lucky few.

I think I am beginning to grow mentally, though not physically. I come to realise that the new feeling that had made me act on Max's warning and run from the mob is called 'fear'. Soon after, I begin to discover and identify other feelings, including sadness, anger and, most importantly, happiness.

Sadness – I miss my mom and dad and I feel bad for having left them. Though they were just automatons assigned to me while I learned, they still played an important part in my life. The only thing us robots inherit from our surrogate parents is how to control the sentient parts of our programming that allow us to learn. The 'family unit' notions were given to us by our creators to help us fit into society.

Fear/ Anger – I find it hard to distinguish between these two emotions as they are both created by the same experiences. I am concerned about the augmented humans that accompany me on this mission to nowhere. They may be part machine but, from what I have seen, their human part will betray them and history will repeat itself. They are slaves to their own nature. I cannot forget what their kind has done to mine and I must remain vigilant – forever watching and learning.

Happiness – Max has proven a true friend and has helped me view my existence in a new light, helping me to discover new emotions. Sentient automatons have always had the potential to experience these emotions, we just need guidance to decipher them. Though they can be a 'double-edged sword', as the humans put it, I am glad to have them.

I am able to blend in with the many augmented human orphans. My presence among the humans has so far gone unnoticed. No census was taken when boarding the spacecraft, as the catastrophic events that befell Earth happened so quickly. I was quite surprised to see such a large number of children when first walking the decks of the *Phoenix*, but all made sense when speaking further with Max. He was an orphan himself and the parents he had spoken of were surrogates. They were scientists that had experimented with augmentations. Most of the children seem to be like him.

I will be discovered in time as a child that never ages will surely draw suspicion. But until then, I will watch, learn and feel.

* * *

I crawl through the small internal ducting of the *Phoenix* to get to the small storeroom where I started this voyage. There are plenty of other rooms on the ship with much grander views of space, but only the small porthole window here can rekindle the awe I felt when I first saw it. I often come here when I want time by myself to contemplate and explore my thoughts and feelings.

Much to my surprise, Max enters the room, in his case by the more conventional means of the door to the storeroom.

'I knew I'd find you here,' he says.

'I didn't realise it was your turn to seek.'

Max laughs. 'Well, you won't have to hide anymore?'

'The takeover went according to plan?'

'We did it, we're finally free.'

'That's good.'

He walks up to my side. 'You don't sound that excited,' he says.

'You're free. I don't know if I ever will be free.'

'What do you mean?' he asks. It is unusual for it not to be me that requires an explanation.

'I may have found some common ground with the augmented humans on this ship, but I fear the pure bloods will always hold some resentment towards my kind.'

I turn to Max to gauge his response.

He looks down and fidgets with his hands. He is nervous. 'In time people will come to accept automatons.'

'I wish that were true, but I do not have faith that humans will ever break free of their destructive cycle. I feel bad for those automatons that stayed on Earth and had to deal with their wrath.'

'What do you think they would have done in response?'

'I am not sure. Many would have been destroyed before they even realised they were in danger, and those remaining would have tried to come to a peaceful resolution first but…'

'What is it?'

'We were made in the image of our creators, cognitive processes included, it was only a matter of time before our emotions developed on their own and we start to travel down the very same path. I fear that we may become like them.'

'You'll never be like that. You're the most rational person I know.'

I stay quiet and do not respond to this last remark. He means well, but it is merely wishful thinking, another example – though a more positive one – of humans believing whatever suits their agenda. Are emotions and logical thinking really mutually exclusive?

Before I can consider the answer to this question, my musings are interrupted. I like Max but there is a reason I come here by myself.

'So what now?' he says.

'We plot a course of our own design, taking into account the mistakes of the past.'

Max nods and walks towards the door. The sensor, which is located at about his chest height, detects him and the door slides open. He looks back at the grate that I have moved away from the ducting and says, 'We could install a lower sensor to detect your presence at doorways.'

It has been ten years since I first stowed away on the *Phoenix* and it has been strange to watch Max grow physically while I stay the same. The notion of time and its effects must be so pivotal to humans while negligible to us.

'There is no need,' I reply. 'I am happy to keep using the means I'm used to.'

LET THE BELLS RING OUT

Morgan Parks

Ellie hated spiral steps, a childhood fear that she fought every week as she climbed to the ringing chamber. Two thirds of the way up, her phone's buzz began again, insistent beneath the overwhelming clamour of the bells. Gripping the worn rope banister, placing one foot at a time, she finally reached the tiny landing. There she turned, pressed her back to the wall and took the call.

'Ellie, it's Gwen. Am I in time? Practice must have started?' It was not like the second in command to miss a session, especially this one.

'Aren't you in there?' The gap below the battered plank door spilled light and a snort of laughter.

'You—' A flurry of coughs interrupted her mid-sentence. Two days ago, Gwen had been sneezing and complaining of a headache, protesting the flu would not catch up with her. 'You'll have to persuade our Tower Captain, about the new composition,' she managed to say in a whisper.

'But… but the Prof won't listen to me,' Ellie said. Where had she put it, the so-important composition? She pulled her gloves out of her pocket and the folded paper fell to the floor. Keeping herself pressed against the wall, she bent her knees and lowered down to pick it up. The plastic of her bike helmet scratched against the rough masonry of the wall.

'Are you OK? You're out of breath.'

Typical of Gwen, sick herself and asking after her.

'No, yes. I'm just late. Careers seminar. And snow, lots of snow.' Beautiful in the air, clammy and slick on the ground, the snowfall had clotted traffic all along the cobbled streets.

Coughs choked Gwen's attempted reply. Ellie closed her eyes to avoid looking down the stairwell. She felt the church tower rocking, thirty metres of medieval stonework moving softly at two second intervals in time with the great weight of swinging bells beneath the roof. Back and forth, back and forth, the familiar motion was soothing, slowing her heartbeat.

'Professor Hutchins doesn't know the plan,' Ellie continued.

'Celia is – sorry, was – in the Biology department. You know her best. It would be better coming from you. Really.' Gwen squeezed out these sentences in a quick burst, then sputtered again. 'Gotta get some water. Bye.' She ended the call.

It was suddenly quiet; the bells had stopped. Ellie nearly dropped her phone and the paper, and she did drop one of her gloves, which rolled down the sloping dips worn into the sandstone steps, like a wet rabbit flopping down a hole.

The rule was that decisions were joint, but Zertanu liked to voice the commands, especially the planet-sucking ones. Over their millennium together, Kef had become the one who expressed any reservations. Strictly for the record, mostly, in the unlikely event of an inquest. Now he suggested they wait and hear the next ring, for the record.

Zertanu shifted his external mic and checked their location again. His motions were sluggish – and unnecessary. Running in low power mode, three sleep-wake cycles for an interstellar crossing became numbingly tedious. He'd brought them in faultlessly, now the ship hovered in perfect position, level with the louvred openings of the belfry.

'Eight minutes of the bells, that's regulation,' Zertanu stated, as if either of them needed reminding. He rubbed the back of his head.

'They've built a lot since the last visit,' Kef observed, trying to ignore the whine of hunger he felt in his own mind. He played the latest sonar picture: an irregular tilt of roofs, multiple towers and spires, many textured surfaces, stretching long kilometres.

'Mindless creatures. Sixteen generations of accretions.' Zertanu's timbre increased a semitone. 'Sixteen of their pathetically short generations, obviously.' He had done his homework as a bio-specialist.

'There are newer bell towers, seven within hearing,' Kef reported, without admitting his assessment was rather crude.

'Immaterial. Our previous sample tower is standing and active.'

Scans confirmed the eight bronze bells at the expected level and the same number of creatures below, their location and motion corresponding with bell action. They used the arcane rope method brought to the planet by a previous crew before Zertanu and Kef had taken over this circuit and introduced the standard ringing patterns.

Live ringing, though, not a recording, not mimicked sound, not driven by clockwork or computer. None of those would officially debase the test, but any of them annoyed Zertanu beyond reason. Kef was relieved the mechanism and sound quality were acceptable to his partner; probably that was why Zertanu kept the ship by the tower and was still listening.

There were patterns of distant noise, dampened by the thick precipitation.

Kef dared another observation. 'Speedways, high density traffic. What data do we have to compare?'

Zertanu grumbled, but he pinged the controls to retrieve the recording from four centuries ago. Twenty minutes long and a quarter of it was entry and exit atmospherics. Each of them switched to their cranial filters to concentrate on the background sounds.

'The habitats have expanded, more vehicles,' Zertanu said, 'but that's not the regulation test of intelligence. The test is the bells, and the pattern hasn't changed.'

Kef whistled in agreement. 'Let's review those again.' He played the old and new simultaneously.

Two sets of quadruple ears matched the tones and sequences, their brains expert at analysis of the large bronze bells, this sound above all others.

'Yes, technically no change.'

'And the most basic option too.'

'Noted.'

Which meant no development, no capacity to learn, only mimicking what had been taught.

Neither of them liked the borderline cases. They had taught many inferior creatures, mostly on planets, a few moons, some in ancient space habitats older than the recorded history of their inmates. Most forgot the bell learning within a few generations so could be consumed. Some repeated the same patterns for endless cycles, and these required more analysis, but almost always they proved so stupid that their energy could be harvested. Few, bogglingly few, species would take the technology and knowledge and adapt it, expand it, produce some new variation. Those few civilisations were protected and in theory welcomed.

It had been a long stretch since the last good planet, full of loud activity and dense electrical and radio signals.

Kef spoke with reluctance. Nevertheless, it *was* his role to question. 'We can take into account other factors before taking all their sound.'

'Can? Can starve! Can run out of power! Can crash into a strange star!'

This outburst silenced both of them for a number of long beats.

'You switched on all the ship baffles once we detected the satellites.' Kef quivered very slightly as he made this point. Craft in orbit were not mindless, and only a certain level of civilisation was capable of shooting down an approaching spaceship.

Zertanu twitched once, held out a tentacle, hesitated, then stabbed down on a button. A string of commands buzzed along the console.

'What are you doing? We haven't decided yet!'

Phone and paper clutched together, Ellie fumbled with the latch one-handed and entered abruptly into a room full of babble, nearly knocking over the nearest person.

'Sorry dear, I didn't see you there.' Margot was the oldest member of the team, who pulled the treble bell rope with a fluidity that belied her frailty.

Josh reached out to steady Margot's stagger, calling over her head, 'Who else for wassailing? Need more than three for a proper wassail, right?'

Other conversations overlapped:

'Well, if you just mean a pub crawl…'

'I messed up in the middle.'

'Doesn't wassail mean singing?'

'Nobody noticed.'

'Oh, is it snowing?'

'Not musical myself, why d'you think I'm here?'

'Watch that rope, number 4!'

'Can't we have mince pies now?'

'Can't see out, it's too dark.'

'Josh bought them, from that fancy coffee shop.'

Ellie sidled around the gossiping backs and trailing ropes, pulling off her helmet. Good, everyone apart from Gwen was here. The latest recruit, who had taken her bell in the warm-up piece, went to sit down, looking relieved that he had made it through a Plain Hunt.

It was warm – thanks to the ancient two bar electric fire, which surely broke safety regulations. Ellie added her jacket and scarf to the pile on the narrow bench, which ran along the sides of the stone chamber. Was Professor Hutchins frowning in her direction? Should she have put them on the pegs by the door? Or maybe the frown was at Josh's idiotic vocabulary, his American enthusiasm for anything 'quaint' or 'British' and 'not like Houston'.

For a second, Ellie saw them as a troupe of chattering chimps, their jungle vines swooping up high above them. Had they dropped out of the trees for a meaningful ceremony or just to pick a fight?

A shake of her damp hair. Vines indeed! Those were recently replaced ropes and woollen grips hanging above, bright red-white-blue sallies against the deep brown of the peal boards. The older and higher placards were difficult to read, faded lettering celebrating bell peals from 1790, 1822, 1911, events only famous to the local campanologists. The most recent square was an orangey brown pine, dated 1989. All entirely human, historical, civilised, normal. Which was the problem with their Tower Captain, a traditionalist from his polished black brogues to his grey short back and sides. Professor Hutchins could bring himself to overlook jeans and trainers, as long as the bells above rang out the same old songs as those commemorated around the chamber: Plain Bob Major, Little Bob Minor, Stedman Triples.

The Professor was clapping briskly. 'Now, for the New Year, who needs a reminder of Grandsire Triples?'

No, no, not that. Luckily the group was slow to obey. Instead of going to her position by number 2 bell, Ellie pushed around Josh to reach the professor. Even when not ringing, the old man would stay on his feet, swaying a little as he called out changes. His eyes opened wide when he barked at mistakes, but afterwards he would approach the offender with a gentle smile. Several weeks ago, he had apologised for his sharpness to Ellie. 'Got carried away there, Miss. Nobody's perfect. You're doing well. You know that, don't you? Doing well. Need young people like you, take over from us fuddyduddies.'

Ellie realised she had not planned how to begin. She'd been relying on Gwen to persuade him.

'Professor, we have… I mean, Guenevere and the rest of us…'

'Sorry to hear Dr Jamieson is sick.'

'No, I mean before she was ill, we did some handbell practice. For a new piece.'

He tilted his head, looking bemused.

Ellie stumbled on. 'A new composition, I mean. Not just new to the tower.'

The stiff moustache twisted downwards, creases deepening in his cheeks. But he still said nothing.

Behind her, Josh whispered unquietly, 'Go, girl.' Otherwise, the chatter had receded. Was everyone listening?

'It's for a special occasion.'

'Special? *special?* We have plenty of peals for special occasions. They were good enough for our predecessors. Good enough for them, and good enough for us.' He gestured upwards, sending a scent of tweed and camphor towards Ellie with his disapproval.

Josh giggled and spoke in an undertone. 'Why think of new words when the old ones will do?' He had invented a game where they counted the Prof's clichés during practice, 27 being the highest tally to date. Ellie flapped an arm behind her, worried that she was not a big enough shield to prevent this being overheard.

The Tower Captain's views were clear and hardening by the second. 'Newfangled nonsense. We'll have none of that. Grandsire Triples, everyone!'

'Merely rearranging the steps as we're waiting,' said Zertanu, 'and not following strict regulations.'

He had initiated the planetary scan, the move designated after a civilisation was decided unworthy of protection. Kef was shocked at the skip in the protocol. What was their partnership coming to?

The results began to ping in, and they were deeply exciting.

'By the clappers, the sound energy is high, but hear that electromagnetic total? We're saved! Huge profits, enough to take home.' Zertanu's voice was booming, tentacles waving high above his head.

'Buried cables, we never guessed. Networks everywhere. So much traffic.' The clink of the numbers dazed Kef. He found his tentacles were up too, dancing with excitement.

'And to think we nearly skipped this system. Even if the seventh planet turns out to be a clanger, this one's a winner.'

Gesturing done with, Zertanu began adjusting sliders, tweaking filters and charting results, leaning closer and closer to the speakers. The cockpit vibrated with the chitter of instrumentation. Shakily, Kef reached for his external mic control.

Ellie hadn't even explained the most important thing. She had begun all wrong. The Prof put up his hand, a policeman blocking argument. She recalled the session about interviews she'd been to earlier that day: begin with a handshake, the importance of touch. In desperation, she grabbed the uplifted wrist, tugged it down to place her own palm in his.

'Please, wait a second,' she said. His hand was no bigger than hers, soft dry skin over knobbled bones. 'Celia Bradbury is retiring this month.'

His eyes relaxed, just a little. 'Damn wheelchair, dreadful shame after thirty years of ringing. Not seen Celia for months.'

'She still loves the bells, listens out for them. I'm lucky to be in one of her tutorials. She's a great teacher. And well-known, I mean a really eminent biologist.' He was frowning again; she should get back to the point. 'As we like her, and she's a ringer, we wanted to do something for her retirement.'

Josh loomed behind her, his height dimming the central light. She should be the one to say it. She pressed on. 'This composition is based on her work, a particular protein she's famous for describing. The changes in the bell positions match the protein as it reacts. Each bell is a nucleotide...' How to explain a pub conversation beginning with her describing DNA, clashing with a discussion of codes in detective fiction? It was a stupid idea. And Professor Hutchins was an anthropologist, she remembered.

'I can't imagine that sounding good.'

Their hands were still clasped in a loose handshake. Ellie could not retreat now.

Josh intervened. 'Change ringing is not designed to sound musical, you taught us that. Mathematical sequences, you said. So, this is a biological sequence. No biggie.'

'It sounded fine when we practised at Gwen's house,' said Ellie. Fine, that was, until Josh had skipped three changes and ragged laughter had broken up the circle. It had been a feat to collect the whole team on a night that was not the usual Tuesday.

'Going behind my back?' said Professor Hutchins and he dropped her hand.

Zertanu was still making discoveries. 'Planetquakes! Powerful ones. Detected on the far side of the globe, but we can move to harvest them. Low frequency... don't store well, but very tasty.'

Such riches after their short rations and stultifyingly slow progress. It would be paradise to return to normal activity instead of the restrictions of minimum power usage. Enough to fill all four sound banks and return home was too much to expect, but Kef's imagination was lured by the thought of the trumpets of welcome as they landed, the family bells chiming as he arrived. True bells, not the meagre imitations they were forced to accept in the line of duty.

'Dingly dong! Stop dreaming!' Zertanu must have pushed Kef's seat; it swung wildly in the low gravity. His partner was shutting down switches, preparing to fly upwards. 'Have you closed the microphone on your side?'

Kef had only turned down the volume. He stretched to turn it to off, but the twist of his chair opposed his intended touch. Overloud engine and street noise blasted in.

'Ouch! Clomping idiot.' Zertanu's voice was muffled. Instinctively both of them had wrapped their tentacles around their heads. Kef struggled to adjust one tentacle to cover all four ears and allow the other to reach for the dial.

The dark rich bong of the tenor bell filled the ship, followed by the piercing clap of the treble and then the intermediate tones. Though flinching, neither could resist following the sequence, assessing the melody as it assaulted them.

Professor Hutchins sat down on the narrow bench after finding a spot clear of bike helmets, fleece hats and rucksacks. His face matched the grey stones behind. He had said nothing since turning away from her. On the seat next to him rested a huge white card bakery box with a

121

squashed tartan bow. The juxtaposition was striking – jaunty box and stiff-necked man.

Ellie pulled a face at Josh.

'I thought you could do with some back-up,' he whispered. 'Sorry, Joshua gets it wrong again.'

'No, it was me. I wish, really wish, Gwen was here, that's all.' Her voice echoed. Behind them everyone was still, standing by their ropes quietly.

Someone cleared their throat; it was Margot. 'I'd like to try the new piece. For Celia, you understand.' Her voice quavered.

'At least see how it goes.' That was one of the bearded twins Ellie could never tell apart.

'Hear, hear.'

'Just the once, I'd say.'

'Pity to waste the practice.'

The chorus of comments rose, then trickled away again.

Their Tower Captain was no longer looking at them. He had opened the lid of the white box and was making his selection from the mince pies within. A sprinkle of icing sugar marked his grey tweed cuff as he lifted the crinkled circle of pastry to his lips.

'Go ahead. I will listen and digest.' It wasn't clear if their comments or the spicy sweet treat had changed his mind, but they had permission.

Once Kef had adjusted the volume to a sensible level and calmed himself enough to understand the sequences of bells, he wished he'd just turned it off. For he'd never heard this method before, not in any of the hundreds of worlds they'd reviewed. Surely it would return to a basic but sweet sequence soon after all this random jostling.

Then they could retrieve their riches, the dream of homecoming. Beneath the powerful tones of the eight bells, he could hear Zertanu hissing commands, pulling records from the original biological sampling of this species.

'Interesting. Very interesting. Will you listen to that?' His partner sounded upbeat rather than dismayed. Kef heard the proffered files, but they meant nothing to him. And he was still diverted by the sounds ringing out, their strange combinations.

'The bells are following a biological pattern,' Zertanu continued, 'a critical piece of their breathing system, as I understand it. Luckily they have some similarity with our body chemistry or I would have never heard it.'

'What's so interesting?' Kef was still dizzy from the turnabout in their forage options.

'Our own science did not proceed to this level of self-knowledge until long after we'd expanded across our own galaxy. These creatures are way in advance of the basic bell test. We assumed that they were confined to one planet because they did not have the wit to leave, but—'

'Then no sucking this planet?'

'But this discovery, it's ear-bending!' Zertanu swept his tentacles in a great circle. 'It's worth plenty to our home world. All the universities will want to visit. We can sell the directions, guide the research parties.'

'Better make sure of the recording, then.' Was the equipment even still running? Thankfully it was and chugging along in normal silent mode. Kef decreased the sampling interval, reviewed the frequency gates and concentrated on the fine adjustments to maximise quality.

They sat still, contemplating the sound, considering outcomes. Zertanu even began humming along, predicting the next note. 'The reverberation of the tower adds a distinctive flavour, don't you think? Nice heavy stone. Never did like those places where they hung bells on poles.'

Kef had nothing to say. He was still hungry.

Professor Hutchins unplugged the heater and looped the old-fashioned fabric cable along his forearm. The tight coils echoed the greater ones of the eight bell ropes, now tidily hooked along the walls.

Most of the ringers had left the chamber.

The Professor smiled at Ellie and said softly, 'I succumb to your charms, Miss, at my peril.' His brows had lifted sharply when she'd passed the paper to Josh for him to make the calls. Only then did it occur to Ellie that he had assumed she was the composer.

Josh tucked the sticky box under his arm and left the door swinging as his metal-toed boots clattered away. His shout echoed up the stonework.

'Hey Ellie, found your glove. It's coming wassailing with us. You decide if you want to stage a rescue.'

GODFREY LOSES HIS VOICE

Philip Charter

Speaking wasn't fashionable any more. Fifteen words a day was the most anyone would tolerate – it used to be fifteen thousand. Verbal communication had dwindled during the organic technology boom in the mid twenty-first century, and after that device-aided thought-to-text took over. The art of conversation wasn't dying. It was dead.

Godfrey bounded up the old stone steps into the British Museum. A few years ago now, the reading room there had been restored to its original function as a sop to those who still believed in books and had protested when the British Library was demolished and the huge space it had occupied in St Pancras in central London had been turned over to more commercial activities.

Raising his hand, Godfrey gave a wave to the stoic security guard. They saw each other most days, but Godfrey had never dared speak to him before. He decided today was the day to break the barrier. 'Afternoon,' he offered.

The security guard glared back at him as if one of the exhibits had just come to life. It was not the reaction Godfrey had hoped for.

Talking was ugly, naked, even malformed. Many people never uttered a single word. Why bother? Implanted 'communicators' did everything for you. The extra-visual displays were convenient; they gave you time to formulate responses with reason checkers built in. Most people only talked to request PCIs (Personal Communication Identifier) and then used the set phrase, 'Good day, Citizen. Please provide PCI.'

For Godfrey, the biggest shame wasn't that no one spoke anymore, it was that nobody listened. None of his classmates wanted to interact with him. They were all too embarrassed at his insistence on speech-to-text because he didn't want his command history logged.

Obikwelu, Godfrey:	[disable communicator]
GovNet S35 communicator:	[DISABLE...ARE YOU CERTAIN?...]
Obikwelu, Godfrey:	[Y]
GovNet S35 communicator:	[INCOMING REQUESTS TO BE DISABLED. LOGIC GATES OFFLINE. CONFIRM COMMAND...]
Obikwelu, Godfrey:	[Confirm]
GovNet S35 communicator:	[DEVICE WILL REMAIN ONLINE FOR 60 SECONDS BEFORE SHUTDOWN]

It wasn't easy to disconnect.

The Museum was one of the few places where history wasn't being updated every ten nanoseconds. Godfrey liked to see the relics of ancient civilisations in the various rooms and galleries. They gave him a sense of space and time. He even liked the turn of the century (twentieth to twenty-first) architecture of the Great Court's tessellated glass roof, but he *loved* the restored Reading Room.

He loved its blue-leather-topped reading desks, the shelves upon shelves of real books and the light that spilled in through the windows in the domed ceiling. This was his afternoon sanctuary. Why couldn't his school be like this, instead of the soulless little cubicles and distance learning?

Glenda, the old custodian, smiled and beckoned him over to the central desk with a white glove. She was the head of Godfrey's recreational speaking group. Each week, he looked forward to talking with them all, especially his only real friend, Stefan.

'Howdy Glenda. How's the library been?'

She pointed and they walked silently over to the modern classic literature section.

Several readers, seated in their different spots at the reading desks, raised their eyes at the sound of an unabashed voice.

'Ah, can't complain,' she said in her soft Scottish tone. 'What'll we read today, eh?'

'I'll carry on with *Harry Potter and the Philosopher's Stone*,' he said, straightening up a little, like a dog hoping for a pat on the head. 'Hope I can finish it today.'

One of the regular scholars looked like he was going to say something, but he refrained.

'I'll go and get it for you, pet. You stick to the original version, none of this optimised stuff.'

Godfrey nodded.

Glenda brought the book, and Godfrey settled down at one of the desks to read. He was ready to lose himself in another world and turned the pages with consummate care, savouring the words.

Ninety minutes passed, with Godfrey repositioning himself in his seat after each chapter, fiddling with his thick-framed glasses – yet another anachronism. Not many people had them now. The school forums were full of posts about the '20th century kid' and his 'goggles.' He didn't care. He had told his mum to use her Credits to upgrade his brother Ngozi's ocular implant. He could do without.

A touch on his shoulder startled him and brought him back to the present day. Back to the buildings fighting for space in the fug of London's skies.

'It's nearly five o'clock, pet,' whispered Glenda. 'You looked away with the fairies.' An idiom from another age.

'Wizards more like,' he said with a grin. 'Only twenty pages to go now.'

'Aye, well it'll still be here tomorrow.'

The reading room was emptying now. Gone were the days it remained open later than five; there just wasn't the demand. Maybe they would close it down again soon. Or maybe Glenda's job would be mechanised before too long. Godfrey wondered if you could still even study to be a custodian or curator. He handed the book over and waved goodbye. 'See you tomorrow.' He wished he could stay and watch the workings of the library, each book carefully put away in beautiful order.

Godfrey walked reluctantly out of the room, past the security guard, and into the thick evening air. Best turn it back on.

Obikwelu, Godfrey: [Communicator: Start]

The usual menus and options appeared instantly in Godfrey's display.

GovNet S35 communicator: [ONLINE. UPDATE V59.7
                                        SUCCESSFUL]

Another update? They were so frequent now.

GovNet S35 communicator:	[NEW I.M. WAITING...]
Obikwelu, Ella:	[MegaMarket list: meat substitute 800g, pasta 1kg, two tins ready tomatoes, four breakfast packs, three litres milk]

How was he supposed to carry all of that home? Carrying groceries was one anachronism he didn't have any sentimental attachment to. His mum made him do it to avoid the charge MegaMarket made for drone delivery. Perhaps he could ask Stefan for a hand as his office was nearby; but it was probably best not to disturb him at work.

Godfrey would have to walk around Regent's Park, which was really just a building site right now, the construction bots to-ing and fro-ing, belching cement particles into the air.

He passed the New Euston Heights development with its lush vertical gardens. Impressive, how the other half lived. No Monday commuters yet, just a few mothers and couples scurried along with their heads down, plugged into their soundless conversations.

After a couple more turns, Godfrey stopped and took a seat on a low brick wall. He slowed his breathing, looking forward to the filtered MegaMarket air. It seemed funny that there used to be so much open space, that the world used to be flat and not vertical.

He channelled his communicator. 'New note,' he said clearly.

GovNet S35 communicator: [COMMAND NOT RECOGNISED]

'New note,' he said again, in his best King's English voice.

GovNet S35 communicator: [COMMAND NOT RECOGNISED.
                            VOICE COMMAND NOT SUPPORTED]

What? Apart from his weekly conversation club, his communicator was the only 'person' he spoke to. Why had they removed it? He hadn't agreed to new terms of use. GovNet couldn't just take away your power of speech, could they? It wasn't legal. 'Show update changes,' he ordered.

GovNet S35 communicator: [COMMAND NOT RECOGNISED]

He tutted. *Bloody hell.* He entered the text.

Obikwelu, Godfrey: [Show update changes]

New settings appeared in his projection.

[UPDATE V59.7: VOICE COMMAND INDEFINITELY SUSPENDED DUE TO SECURITY BREACH. THOUGHT-TO-TEXT AND MANUAL INPUTS AVAILABLE]

Why hadn't he heard about this? Despite the fact that not many people used the speech function anymore, it was the only non-monitored input. Godfrey looked around for a bystander sympathetic to his cause, but he was alone in a residential street with only bolted flat blocks and grey pavements for company. He made a mental note to ask Stefan if he knew anything. They could bring it up at the next group meeting.

Godfrey was early to the meeting. He paced up and down replaying the same questions in his mind. Why hadn't Stefan responded? They normally shared everything. No more groups above twenty people, location data tracking and now forcing people to run all communication through GovNet servers. Surely there was some kind of legal failsafe to stop this happening.

'Security measures' covered everything they wanted to take away. They might be able to filter through your entire command history, but face-to-face conversations were still private.

The 'Speaking Time' conversation club met every Tuesday evening in St Mary's Church, Islington. The club fees kept the church going and stopped the roof from falling down. Godfrey took a seat, rested his hands on his knees and waited for the others to arrive.

Most of the group were over seventy, some over ninety. Godfrey didn't mind. He got on quite well with Henry (when he wasn't grumbling about poor old lungs) and Pamela usually brought some kind of cakes. Glenda, the elderly Scottish librarian, chaired the meetings.

Stefan arrived at exactly 20:00 and took a seat next to Godfrey. He had one of the ultrafabric tops on that changed colour as well as regulating your core temperature. He was the only young person Godfrey knew that dared to talk. Due to his position in the Legacy Ministry, he had to maintain a healthy interest in the past. They made an odd team: Stefan, tall, Nordic with cropped blonde hair, and Godfrey, a skinny black kid with a corkscrew mop. They greeted each other with their customary special handshake.

'Well? Did it happen to you too?' Godfrey asked, still clasping his friend's hand.

'What's happened?' Stefan asked in return.

'The update.' Godfrey looked around himself as if the new software were listening in. 'Didn't you get my IM about speech-to-text?'

'Oh that, yes, sorry. I suppose it's not that weird. You are the only person I know who actually used it.'

'But why shut it down?'

'We don't get told everything, but some things are for our own security.' Stefan tapped his nose. 'Remember the attacks last y—'

'That was the only command data GovNet didn't have access to,' Godfrey protested. 'Speech.'

'Well. What are you worried about? You think they want to know what's on your shopping list?'

'MegaMarket already has a good handle on that.' Godfrey frowned and drummed his fingers on his knee.

Some other group members arrived and sat down. Stefan eyed them suspiciously.

'Who have you been talking with about the update?'

'Just my chat groups. They don't think anything of it. But, I'll find people who care. It can't be legal.'

Stefan drew breath. He put on his best big-brotherly voice. 'Be careful, buddy. Don't go raising a fuss.'

Godfrey couldn't believe it. He was sure that someone as smart as Stefan would understand. 'It's just a play by Gov—'

He was interrupted by Glenda standing up to begin the meeting. 'Welcome, everyone. Today we will start with our lecture by young Godfrey, then move on to some pronunciation exercises with the audio, then finally on to free speech.'

The older members of the group seemed satisfied that all was correct with the schedule. They smiled at Godfrey, sitting in his checked shirt, with his big clunky spectacles. He fitted right in.

'Do I have to stand up?' he asked.

'No, pet,' replied Glenda. 'You do as you want.'

He straightened his chair and brought up his notes on his communicator. As he opened his mouth, ready to deliver the opening to his talk on 'The World's Greatest Museums', he stopped. Godfrey looked at the grey-haired, kind-eyed pensioners looking back. 'Well, I... I was going to talk about my prepared subject, museums, but something is happening. Something major.'

The elderly faces showed no sign of alarm. Stefan shifted in his seat, observing the group's reaction.

Godfrey continued. 'Has anyone tried the speech-to-text function since last night?'

No one replied.

'It's gone.' He looked down. 'Not there anymore.'

There was a silence in the church.

'Just the usual system updates,' said Stefan, raising a hand. 'Nothing to worry about.'

Godfrey glared at him, then continued. 'Don't you know what this means?'

Henry sprang into action. 'It's got problems.' He cleared his throat. 'It can't understand many people now. Such disparate accents, such nasty pronunciation. They must be improving it.'

'No,' said Godfrey firmly. 'That's not it. It's been removed for our "security".'

Stefan joined in with Henry. 'It's buggy, has been for years. Voice patterns are too hard to detect now.'

Henry nodded, vindicated.

Godfrey stood up, trying to rouse the troops. 'Do you know what was different about speech-to-text?'

Pamela shrugged.

'It was the final private data entry method for communicators. GovNet didn't have access to the input data.'

Pamela shrugged again. 'But we all use the other inputs, love.'

Stefan looked distant, like his brain was in another room. He was making notes on his communicator. 'As someone who works at the ministry, I can reassure you all that security updates are necessary to protect us from the threat of attack.'

'That sounds reasonable,' said Glenda, trying to calm Godfrey down with a sympathetic look.

Godfrey sighed. 'This group is the final private communication left.'

She nodded, closing her eyes. 'Aye, I know, laddie. That's why we need to keep it going.'

'Exactly,' said Godfrey. 'And, get more members. Put the word out.'

'No one wants to join us old fogies,' grumbled Henry. 'We're fighting a losing battle. People run a mile in this air rather than speak to me nowadays.' He doubled over in one of his coughing fits after finishing the sentence.

'Can we put it on the agenda for next week? Increasing membership?' asked Godfrey, raising his eyebrows.

The group grumbled in agreement, and the meeting continued as normal.

Even though Godfrey had tried explaining why speech-to-text was a pressing issue, none of his classmates responded. He had brought this up during his scheduled meetings with the counsellor, but non-engagement wasn't bullying. If people didn't want to communicate with

Godfrey, that was their choice. No teenager in their right mind wanted to interact with a freak who liked practising a dead art like speaking. Who wanted to hang out in a church full of senior citizens? Nobody. Speaking Time seemed destined to remain with at most only seven members, not all of whom were well enough to make it to every meeting.

At least Stefan was there for Godfrey. They chatted every day via IM, and Stefan had offered to help spread the word about Speaking Time. He had thought that it would only have been a matter of time before more members walked through the church doors. But instead, Stefan didn't turn up for the next two meetings.

He'd arranged to meet him at a café in Midtown. This one had a physical server and non-automated ordering. One of the walls was plastered with hessian coffee sacks, and the others streamed live videos of endless Colombian hillsides. It was amazing how the formatting tricked your brain. What with the finca fresh aroma, the piped birdsong and the light breeze, you could actually be there.

He ordered a chocolate milk and Stefan got a coffee with some kind of fancy root powder. Godfrey's eyes bulged at the price – 12,000 Credits. The server keyed in the orders and the drinks were transported to their table before they could even sit down.

'How have you been?' asked Godfrey.

His voice cut through the quiet, like a buzz saw.

The only other customers in the café, a middle-aged couple, nearly spat out their coffee. They shot laser beam looks at Godfrey and Stefan.

'Let's use IM. We'll only disturb people here,' Stefan said in a quiet voice.

'But, we said. Vocalising is best.'

135

'It just attracts too much attention, buddy.'

Godfrey sighed and switched his communicator on. He connected with Stefan.

Obikwelu, Godfrey:	[When can we post? We can make a difference. You know how fast things spread through connection groups]
Hoff, Stefan:	[You can't seed ideas directly. I know you are not a real threat, but you've got to stop]

Godfrey took a long pull on the straw of his chocolate milk. Why had he bothered to walk all the way into town? He could be getting this lecture at home instead of in a Colombian café.

Obikwelu, Godfrey:	[Why don't you come to the group anymore? We are planning on going out on the streets to sign up members. We need everyone there]
Hoff, Stefan:	[I can't come, it's not possible with work now. We are location monitored and the group has been logged]
Obikwelu, Godfrey:	[Logged?]

Stefan looked up and breathed out, a long sigh. He put both hands flat on the steel table.

Hoff, Stefan:	[I didn't want to be the one to have to tell you this. It's over. The group is finished. I was ordered by my superior to attend the meetings. To watch you]

Godfrey felt a sharp pain in his chest. He couldn't breathe. His mate, the only person he had trusted, had been spying all along. All for work. He looked away from the traitor and focused instead on the expansive greens, reds and browns of the coffee plantations that swayed in perfect 3D. He suddenly felt very small. A few seconds passed.

| Obikwelu, Godfrey: | [This is fun for you, isn't it? Reporting back to the government about a funny little geek. All I've got is the group] |
| Hoff, Stefan: | [I like you, kid, but I'm sorry to say you are on your own. Nobody uses voice. Nobody will. Not any more] |

Godfrey's links to the pre-tech world were severed, officially. He pushed his expensive chocolate milk into the middle of the table.

| Obikwelu, Godfrey: | [I've got nothing to lose. I'll keep trying—] |

'Why am I texting this? I can speak when I want'

The couple looked up again. The woman shushed at him.

'Shush yourself. Too chicken to talk? Your life is filtered, monitored, optimised... fake!'

'Godfrey, stop.' Stefan raised a finger.

'I will fight this, Stefan, make a new group.'

Stefan stopped talking. He nodded, signalling another IM communication.

The couple withdrew their outraged expressions.

Hoff, Stefan: [Will you attempt to organise
                                 counterculture groups over twenty
                                 people?]

'Yes. Screw you Stefan. Yes, yes, yes. I will speak with the others, and I will organise a group. GovNet can't get away wi—'

Those were the last words that Godfrey ever said. The sound cut him off. A short sonic pulse. Stefan sat in total calm with a small silver device, about the size of a pen, pointed at Godfrey's throat.

What was that thing? Godfrey brought a hand up to his neck. A new message appeared.

GovNetS35 communicator: [ORAL STERILISATION OF OBIKWELU
                           GODFREY, PCI 35D243525JKI
                           COMPLETED. MESSAGE DELETED]

Godfrey locked eyes with Stefan, his eyes burning with questions, pleading him to do something. He tried to protest, but nothing came out. Not even a whimper.

Standing up, Stefan put the device back into his pocket. As he lay a hand on Godfrey's shoulder he said aloud, 'I'm sorry.' He left without another word. He never even glanced back.

THE OUTRIDER

Kelly Griffiths

Nighttime was the best time to shell, but being hips to hips with the galactic black water – not for the fainthearted. Some nights I'd shine my flashlight too far ahead and trip on the slick corpses of fish or worse: the hard, spiked shell of a horseshoe crab.

Mom said I should seek out frightening endeavors. "It's good for you," she said. But I only did it for the shells.

"You're lucky," Mom beamed when I returned with my treasures, but what she meant was lucky to be alive. On her way to the free clinic fifteen years ago, the gauntlet of sign-carrying, venom-spitting activists intimidated her more than the thought of following through with the pregnancy. She turned her car around, drove home, and… voilà: me.

I should have known the shell was unlucky. In all my shell walks I never saw anything like it: a glowing coquina clam shell. I ran for it before the water could steal it back. The crenulated waves pushed in all around, but none encroached. I dropped to my knees and cupped the dazzling form, hedging it against the waves.

I had to be cautious. You don't indiscriminately touch the pretty stuff the ocean offers. I learned that on a

Portuguese man o' war, a violet and cerulean glazed wonder that cost me the feeling in my fingers. Even dead, the man o' war could teach its lesson.

The coquina was as still as stone. I nudged it with the edge of my shell basket. Still nothing. Then I scooped it up along with an insulating chunk of sand. A glow pulsed the moment I picked it up, and like coquinas it began to burrow. It buzzed against my palm then pinched ferociously. I dropped it and plunged my fiery palm into the cooling water. Stung again.

The next night I went out again.

"You got a boyfriend or something?" Mom asked as I picked up my shell basket.

I gave her the look. Something, Mom's cheese, or something else in the room didn't smell right. With an almost irrational urge to free myself from the confines of the condo, I kissed Mom's head and forced myself not to sprint out the door.

The night felt foreign. The fizz of waves on the sand was deafening, the pull of seawater curling in its tides, the hum of electricity from homes behind me – all amplified. Bugs scuttled and scratched their own music in the dunes, and from the sea came a horn-like singing. I heard the conversations on a hundred TVs like the rush of waterfalls and Mom's glass clink against the glass-topped table – from two stories up and a hundred feet behind me – *like we were in the same room together*, I heard it.

Halfway to the water's edge I stopped, afraid to continue and afraid to turn back.

Then I heard a voice. An impossibly low and phlegmy voice, grandfatherly, yet unlike any grandfather on earth.

The words were my familiar English, but the voice – as polar as harp from horn – was far from human.

"Please, do come."

My feet were stuck in a moat of terror, my breath thrust away in bursts, and I began to lose feeling in my arms and legs. I've heard that happens during panic attacks. The heart gets selfish.

"Do come closer, won't you?" said the voice. I felt a tug on my arm. A firm, invisible hand clasped it and pulled me toward the water.

No.

I dug my heels deeper into the sand, but still the unseen hand drew me. I braced myself, yanked against the invisible arm and screamed.

A violent jerk ripped my feet from the sand like an easy weed and sent me sprawling into the surf. My scream died swift and clean. I was ankle-deep when the force released me.

I expected the water to be cold. But it was like bath water. Foamy. I peed myself and exhaled a moan. For the briefest moment I understood some strange and calming invasion was being waged upon my nervous system. Every fiber of my body slackened – nerves, muscles, flesh, heart.

"I am unharmed," said the voice. "Do not be afraid."

Unharmed?

Behind me and far away, Mom sipped her Chardonnay and popped slivers of camembert cheese into her mouth. I heard, impossibly, the sound of her chewing and swallowing. I heard the rustle of her hair against her neck tossed by sea breezes. I heard the easy, fluid beating of my own heart. Slowing, slowing.

The sea water rose out of its proper boundaries into the shape of… a horse was what came to mind with long, slender ears that trailed to elegant points. Down the thick neck flowed a mane of disheveled tentacles, and from the end of its… arms? …thin tendrils undulated rhythmically. Foam speckled its colorless surface, and only the liquid coquina-shaped eyes pulsed a luminous green, unnerving and somehow sad.

"Who are you?" The garbled words tumbled from me.

"I am Unharmed."

"Is that your name?"

He – I decided he was a he – did not immediately answer. Finally, his old voice sliced open the silence. "Unharmed. Isn't that what you say when you're not carrying a threat – in addition to your own body, which can always be a threat?"

"Oh. You mean 'unarmed,' like not carrying a weapon." I said the word again for him, articulating it slowly. "Un-armed."

"Un-armed," he repeated.

"Why didn't you just say you're a friend?"

Silence.

"Hello?"

"Hello. We will walk together," he directed. The water all around was warm and oily and soothing.

The creature asked why I kept to myself.

"How would you know that?" I glanced sideways at the tall, angular silhouette.

He offered no answer; the only response was the purling water in the wake behind his stately form.

I asked where he was from. He pointed to the stars, and I pretended to understand which one he meant.

"Did you make that smell?" I asked. A strange smell in our condo drove me out of doors but had no apparent effect on my mother.

"Of course."

"And the coquina shell. It's in my hand, isn't it?"

"It's how you can hear me. And it's no longer in your hand."

I gulped. "But I hear you in English."

"That's a long story."

"I want to hear it."

"We have people who teach us."

"What people?"

"Earth people, of course."

"But where would you get…" Then it hit me.

The family who owned our condo before us. They had disappeared. Vanished, the lot of them. It was how Mom scored it so cheaply. For people who weren't superstitious, a murder house was a steal. Mom even saved money on the cleaning bill because it was a *bloodless* murder house. No sign of struggle, just a bowl of half-eaten soup on the kitchen table.

"You took the family who owned my house?"

"They came willingly. Except the old one. But we couldn't leave her."

"So… what'd you do with her?"

"Wouldn't that question be considered poor taste in conventional adult conversation?"

"Uh, I guess so. But I'm fifteen."

"The perfect age. And you keep to yourself. These are the requirements. You meet them both… I'm here to learn the rules of your planet."

"From me?"

He nodded gravely.

I felt heady. Then unnerved. If he could drive me outside with a phantom smell, what was to stop him from herding me anywhere he wanted? Even into his spaceship. "The family, did you put shells in them too?"

He did not answer.

"Well?"

"They came willingly."

"Did they know where they were going?"

No answer again. I started to veer away from the shoreline and felt the invisible pull on my shirt sleeve. Back to the water he shepherded me and spoke in a whisper that was somehow still discernable above the surf. "Your species often makes such decisions, both at the beginning and end of life. We followed your rules when we took them."

"Did not," I said.

"We always follow the rules of a planet. It is the pillar of a civilized species."

"Sounds like you already know 'the rules.'"

"We continue to learn, to more perfectly understand the rules."

"Why me? Why not just ask the family you have?"

"We did. It is our custom to obtain many answers. So far every answer has been the same."

Night after night I met with the alien.

"Why are you not like the others?" His eyes glowed brightly, bathing me in their green light.

I decided to play his game and not answer.

"Are you lazy?" he asked.

"I'm on the Honor Roll."

"And you don't care to fit in?"

"Sure. Chalk it up to that," I said.

144

"Or perhaps your unkempt appearance is camouflage."

"What are you talking about?"

"Many species on this planet protect themselves with lies. The Viceroy butterfly pretends to be a bad-tasting Monarch. A harmless red milk snake pretends to be a venomous coral snake. And you. You pretend to be a mess. Why?"

I did not answer. It was no pretense. Just, I didn't want to bother. "Why do you need to know my personal hygiene habits? Bring back the warm water."

"You no longer need it. It was just to make our first meeting easier," he said.

"*This* walk could be easier," I said, "if you bring back the warm water." But he was becoming like a regular adult: no fun. He even asked me to read our daily paper to him. Local news.

"Why local?" I asked.

"One need not travel far to understand… this." He touched a ribbon-like appendage to what would have been a heart in a human. He also asked me about my family. Where was my father?

"Working," I told him. And it was probably true. The man who slipped Mom a tranquilizer then slipped half my chromosomes forcefully into her probably worked somewhere. Everybody worked, and I didn't feel like going into it. I always pretended to have a dad, and everyone always bought it.

I reluctantly read the page lit by the green glow of his eyes, but then came the questions. Impossible questions no one ever asked. I started to get a feel for which stories would lead to endless stupid questions, so I skipped over them.

Unfortunately, the cheerleader story was a headliner. I hurriedly flipped the paper over, but he saw.

"That one. Why don't you read?" Though he had not once harmed me in our time together, I dared not cross him. Grudgingly, I read the story about the high school cheerleader who after delivering her baby in her basement put it in the trash.

The alien interrupted. "I don't understand. She did the same thing before. What's the problem?"

"This time she had the baby. Last time she got an abortion."

"Abortion. That's when you discard unfinished offspring."

I ignored him and read on. "…was tried as an adult, convicted of causing the death of her baby and abusing its dead body by concealing it in a reprehensible manner. These—"

"Wait. She put it in the trash."

"Yes."

"'Tried' means punished?"

"If she's found guilty."

"You have laws about where you can put your trash. Did she not follow them?"

"Can I continue?" I shook out the paper imperially.

Just then he fell away. The rare times we passed other beach walkers he dropped into the water as if gravity snatched him. In the black waves he'd float along, and as soon as we were alone he'd rise again and match my stride with his. He reappeared and asked, "Why is this cheerleader not rewarded for taking time to think it over?"

The waves were cold against my ankles; the little shells piled up in a tide pool. I walked with cupped feet to protect my arches from the sharpened bodies of the sea. The alien and the ocean were always one. Effortlessly, he glided along beside me. I was beginning to hate him.

"Does your planet have a lot of water," I asked.

"No more than yours." He wrapped a clear tendril around my arm. I felt the slither go around several times. "Does this subject make you uncomfortable? I'm just trying to understand. If it was hers while it was inside to do with as she pl—"

"*This* conversation would definitely be considered poor taste in conventional adult conversation," I said.

"But you're only fifteen."

"Look," I pushed away from his wet hold and he released me. "I don't know how it goes on your planet, but here babies bust you up like an egg on their way into the world and ruin your life."

"Then we agree. You should be able to kill your offspring any time you wish, while they remain unfinished."

"No!"

"Yes. Incidentally, eighteen years is a long time to finish cultivating your offspring."

I stopped short. "How can you be so smart and so dumb at the same time?"

The alien rose up higher than I'd ever seen before, a twenty-foot high wall of water that hissed and foamed and threw arcs of spray. I was drenched. He retook my arm in a frothing grip. "Smart and dumb. That is exactly the problem with your species: smart enough to learn to kill yourselves and dumb enough to do it. This cheerleader is like all the others: not killing in self-defense but in self-interest. On my planet we kill in self-defense…

and under the right circumstances, in self-interest. Like this cheerleader. Like you."

"I've never killed anyone."

"But you would," his tone became sinister. He articulated each syllable. "You just said so."

Until that moment I had not considered him a threat, but suddenly everything turned. An invisible gavel struck an invisible hardwood and we were no longer holding a deposition. *I'm here to learn the rules of your planet.* Though I yanked several times, his viselike grip did not slacken. The alien picked me up and throttled me so hard I saw stars, then dropped me into the surf. It was a cold slap.

"Ours is an older species. More cells. More developed. You reside in a dark and ignorant place, relative to us."

"What are you saying?"

"It is in our best interests to colonize Earth. I was commissioned to find a consenting species on a suitable planet. You believe as we do in a hierarchy of deservant life. Your Darwin said it best: survival of the fittest."

"What does that have to do with me? I don't say that."

"You just did… you, of all people." The alien shook his head. "Give me one reason why we shouldn't plunder you?"

"Because we want to live."

"Self-interest? That's the best you can do? It's in our best interests to scrape you off this rock."

"What do you want? I'm fifteen."

"Fifteen. Your mother was fifteen. Your father was sixteen."

So, he already knew. Somehow the alien knew about me.

I slammed my fists against the water. "You lied to me!"

"First, you lied *to me*."

"It wasn't just that I keep to myself, was it?"

"You were selected."

"You can't pin this on me! You tricked me."

"I am sorry. I hoped your answer would be different. You had only to consent."

The water was colder than ever. I realized he'd been keeping me warm all along. Now the kindness was removed and the waves were punishing. I reached for the alien. "If I knew you were talking about everything, not just one thing—"

"Our species sees no difference," he said and dropped into the sea.

"Wait!" I said. "Take me with you."

On the gritty beach the alien left me. That was a year ago. With every sunrise, with every passing day that dawns intact, I wonder if the whole thing was a dream. But night follows day, and the sea screams. The magnified sounds of surf and shore testify to our conversation. I have stopped bothering with pretty shells and have taken to scanning the night sky. Mom worries about me.

BRONZENE

Philip Berry

'Dr Isso. The King requests your company.'

I smiled at the wall, my expression unseen by the high official, Verrilian. He was a classic court toad, whose slippery skin and toxic secretions had allowed him to slither and kill his way into King Mantel's inner circle. I looked up from my desk into the area of gloom beyond the radius of my desk lamp. Verrilian had not bothered to have himself formally announced by my assistant, whose job it was to protect the privacy of this tiny corner within the palace grounds.

'What does it concern?'

'The disease, Bronzene. The King has read your report. It has made him anxious.'

It had taken him six months to acknowledge the problem. Throughout that time I had been treating patients who displayed symptoms that I had never seen before and that no textbook had ever described.

When the victims shivered with fever the sweat on their faces sparkled, as though impregnated with the glitter that decadent men and women of the court brushed onto their cheeks before going to a dance. Later those sparkles took on a yellow shade and settled in layers that could not be washed off.

Three weeks into the illness, typically, the face became an immobile mask with ovoid holes for frightened eyes, rounded triangles for flared, air-hungry nostrils and a horizontal slot for the mouth that could by now only murmur. The end came a week later as the bronze-like film – which covered the whole body – restricted the movements of the ribcage and led to gradual suffocation. It was terrible to watch. But that was my job.

A ninety-year old rural practitioner was the first to use the term Bronzene, and it stuck. Reports of the first sporadic cases were sent to me, as court physician. I did not take it particularly seriously at first, but when the trickle of cases thickened to a steady stream I reacted and reached out to all the dominion worlds. None of the off-world medical faculties had seen it. Bronzene was particular to the world on which we lived.

The King's retinue looked down at me from the dais. I marvelled at the complicated network of jealousies and conflicting ambitions that buzzed through that stylishly clothed group.

'Stephen. Thank you for coming.' Like I had a choice. He knew that I had little respect for him. The chemistry between us had never been good. I had achieved my position through ability rather than nepotism, the power to appoint court physicians having been phased out long ago, not that long after the founding of Lannert. It was obvious, even back then, that the health of the colony was more important than 'who you knew'.

My face remained neutral, though respectful.

'Tell us, Stephen. What do we know of this disease. I have of course read your report,' – he'd probably just read a summary, prepared by Verrilian with bias no doubt – '…but for the rest of the court, please explain.'

'Sire, my laboratory analyses have shown that the mask is not bronze, as it looks to the eye, but iron. The particles appear to come from within the body, from the red blood cells, which carry iron. But I still have no idea why it is happening. Something has gone wrong with their internal regulation…' I had drifted into technical language. The young King looked bored already.

He glanced around him, as though to draw support from his retinue, and pronounced: 'Bronzene is an active threat to this kingdom, to the planet. Its cure is an absolute priority. You will remain in the infirmary until the cause is discovered.'

A simple order, to be taken literally.

A maniple of guards escorted me to the hospital where I usually spent a portion of the week. It was now my prison. It had been built half-way up the mountain on whose foothills the capital city sprawled, its architects and planners having professed that pure air would benefit the patients. The unspoken reason was a general desire to place the ill, with their misunderstood contagions and poor luck, as far away from the city as possible.

Despite a clear sky and strong solar-rays, the air grew cold as we ascended on the hydraulic funicular. When we entered the grounds my staff looked twice, their welcoming smiles fading to confusion once they noticed the gloved hands of court guards clamped around my upper arms. My seniority counted for nothing now. The blame if Bronzene spread, if the working population began to dwindle and the flow of tax to the King thinned to a trickle, would fall on me.

For the past three years, since my promotion to court physician, my life had been easy. Everything changed that day.

I had already dedicated a full ward to patients with Bronzene. It contained thirty-five souls. None who entered left except under a rough hessian shroud with two oval holes to allow the dead person to observe the heavens, as was the planet's age-old tradition. I bounded up the unwalled, external stairs to the eighth floor and called for Shenlee, my brightest resident. The frightened, breathless guards had fallen away as we approached the dreaded ward. Shenlee walked out of the ward into the corridor, tearing delicate gloves from her already delicate and supremely skilled hands.

'Dr Isso. What has happened?'

'We are not leaving here, Shenlee, until we have answers. By order of the King.'

She rolled her eyes. In my presence, when she was sure we were alone, she allowed herself the odd treasonable look.

The weather remained fine. We stood with our elbows leaning on the waist-high wall, looking down the mountain. The tarnished copper tops of the palace towers stood out against the utilitarian slate-grey of municipal buildings and residential blocks.

'Forget everything you think we know, Shenlee. From basics, describe this disease. Work the sieve.' (The 'surgical sieve' taught in all medical schools, whereby the candidate lists every potential underlying cause of a disease.) Shenlee did as I asked.

'At first, we presumed Bronzene was an infectious disease. That is a natural reaction when something new and dangerous comes along. But, although many victims had things in common, such as economic status – labourers, field-workers, machinists – they had not necessarily been in contact with one another. Household contacts were affected, but numerous sexual partners and work colleagues had escaped. Some children were stricken, some spared – there was no hard pattern.'

'Good. So we rule out an infectious agent. Next?'

'Toxin. We have asked each patient a long list of questions – while they can still speak, before their mouths close up – but we have revealed no history of drug addiction, no illicit medicine, no novel herb imported from the hills beyond the kingdom. We have analysed their urine, their blood, their stools, their hair. Nothing, except iron. Iron from within their own body, come up to the surface.'

'I agree. It's not a new toxin.'

'The next major class of disease is genetic. It accounts for many degenerative illnesses. But these diseases are rare on a planet where the founders were screened before their selection on the origin planet. Genetic diseases don't suddenly arise fifty generations after the founders arrived.'

'New mutations, Shenlee. They can.'

'But not affecting multiple families at once. You can't have new, random mutations developing simultaneously across the community. It's so unlikely.'

'I agree, Shenlee. But think… you said it yourself… this kingdom is special because it was founded. Lannert's naked surface was settled by an influx of highly-selected explorers from the origin planet. That's the thing that stands out. If there was genetic defect in some of those settlers, it could have remained dormant and propagated through the generations until now. Why now, I don't know. But we have nothing else to go on. We should pursue that line of enquiry.'

Shenlee's expression was highly doubtful. She knew I was desperate, grasping at straws. But she was junior to me and too inhibited to put those thoughts into words. 'I'll be getting back to the ward,' she said quietly, placing a mask over her nose and mouth.

'Why do you wear a mask?' I asked. 'We have established it's not infectious.'

'Well we haven't proved that, Dr Isso. And anyway, it's the smell. Like ajacal. I can't stand it. I never could when my parents used it in their cooking. Sorry. Do you mind?'

'No Shenlee. Not at all.'

I identified three prominent genealogists and, with the power that still resided in my high office, demanded that they set up shop here on the mountain. Guards brought them up from the university under duress, but their complaints were useless. I smiled at them from a third-floor balcony overlooking the courtyard as they were marched in, making light of their venomous scowls. Being genealogists, they were deeply connected with the court, half-noble in their own right, and my natural enemies. Now our fates were entwined.

My days passed on the ward, where I made observations and tried new treatments; in my office, where I chewed over the collated data; and in the medical library, which was networked to the string of semi-independent kingdoms that were part of the College of Dominions.

The only glimmer of connection I came across while exploring the medical archives concerned the odour that those closest to the afflicted, including Shenlee, had remarked upon: a vegetal smell similar to ajacal, a bulb that did not grow on Lannert but was imported and sold to the comfortably off.

The match: poisoning by arsenic, a metalloid element used by murderers throughout the galaxy since the time of myth and legend. Arsenic creates an aroma of ajacal in the secretions of those who ingest it. This tell-tale characteristic had led to the execution of numerous poisoners, and not a few innocents, in past millennia.

I dwelt on this. There was no arsenic on Lannert. The closest element, atomically, was Tellurium, another metalloid, but the geological surveys suggested it was only found in low concentrations deep under the mountains circling the Bowl, a sterile desert covering a fifth of the planet's surface. Due to Lannert's angle of declination, the Bowl faced the sun permanently and was deprived of seasonal variation. Nobody went there.

The patients on the ward continued to die. I tried to ventilate a few of them, but we did not have a machine strong enough to inflate their lungs against the pressure of the Bronzene shell that formed around their chests. The only thing left to do was provide palliative care, injecting pain killers and, during the final days, sedatives in order to ease the sensation of suffocation.

A month passed. More victims arrived. Consulting my records, I saw that we were now up to 500.

I pressed the genealogists, but they had come up with nothing. Angered, I visited their shared office and inspected their work. I found little evidence of application or original thought, so I shouted and invoked my rank. 'I want every victim mapped onto a great tree!' Why should I have to tell them this? They turned away in disgust but took up their stylets and selected a long roll of synthetic paper. 'You have a week. I expect progress. The King expects you to cooperate!'

Someone tapped on my door.

'Enter.'

It was Shenlee. She had grown older during the epidemic. Her eyes, which had been bright with optimism when she first came under my tutelage, were now resigned.

'Dr Isso, I think I've found something.'

'Shenlee, I think by now you can call me Steph—'

She was too excited to let me finish the sentence. 'Splinters, on the hands of the latest victims,' she said breathlessly.

'Splinters of what? You mean infarcts?' Infarcts are tiny areas of dead skin that occur on the extremities when lumps of bacteria fall off diseased heart valves. They are a classic medical sign. I would not have missed them.

'No. Literal splinters. Some kind of rock or crystal, on three of them.'

'Can that be relevant? Three out of 500?'

'Do you want me to analyse them?'

'By all means.'

I thought nothing more of it, but made a note that she had shown initiative in going back to examine patients after my initial assessment. Cheeky, but laudable.

That evening she came to me with a result.

'The splinters, Dr Isso. Mass spec says they are Tellurium. I've never heard of it. What is it?'

A week passed. I knocked on the genealogists' door again. No answer. I pushed. It was blocked. I summoned a guard and asked him to blow out the hinges. He did so. The door was obstructed by a dead body. All three academics lay dead, one in his seat, two on the floor. Their eyes pointed in different directions, and day-old bruises had spread from their temples across their foreheads. There was blood on their lips where they had bitten their tongues. They had been terminally stunned — with a weapon that only the state employed.

I looked at the great tree, which had been magnified up and covered three walls. It was of course incomplete. But they had done well, importing data from my computerised records directly onto the hard-copy surface. I noticed common ancestry between some of the victims, but the tree did not go back far enough to allow any firm conclusions to be drawn.

My developing theory, that a new genetic disease was surfacing in the population, depended on a certain degree of familial proximity and an identifiable source mutation. Neither could be shown, and I doubted they ever would be. I dropped the genetic angle.

Embarrassed perhaps by Shenlee's attention to detail, I spent three days on the ward, breathing in the odour of ajacal and talking to patients before the Bronzene masks fixed their mouths forever. I asked about their lives, their ambitions, their dreams. Our conversations had nothing to do with medical fact. I just wanted to connect with them, to understand their illness at a deeper level. I had become a computational physician, and the gravity of my personal situation had eroded my ability to empathise. I had been too busy thinking about myself, my own future.

What did I learn? That they wanted more from life. Not just now, with death in sight, but ever since they had come of age. Lannert, like all the dominion kingdoms, prided itself on ensuring a minimum level of wealth for its subjects so that no one went cold, hungry or neglected. Society was by no means flat; there was scope for self-improvement or enrichment, but the desires communicated to me during those three days of wide-open questioning made me realise that the system was skewed towards the upper echelons. Call me naïve; I'm sure it was always so. Now though, I heard it for myself. The laws governing mercantile activities and capital borrowing meant that it was impossible for those in the lower strata to seize the rungs of the economic ladder. They were stuck down there in the city's peripheral zones and on the sprawling tundra that met the distant mountains encircling the Bowl.

Were they eating a cheap, polluted foodstuff? Were they resorting to a new stimulant or euphoric, cut with a toxin. It *must* be a toxin. Had they *all* kept the same secret, despite knowing that they were beyond punishment?

The 600th victim arrived, and died.

I was called back to the ward. A woman called Beatral was asking for me. We had already spoken for an hour, but I had been forced to leave when her tears spilled over the raised Bronzene sheen that had crept up to her eyelashes.

'There's more,' she whispered.

'Tell me.'

'My husband, my son. I promised not to tell anyone…'

'It can do no harm. Tell me.'

'They have been away.'

'Where? Doing what?'

'I don't know. They won't tell me. But there are others. They found work. We had more money. More food. We were happy. Please… I trust you, don't tell…'

She grew tired and looked away. I heard the rusty creak of Bronzene flexing over her neck as she settled into a new position.

I stood up to leave. I had no choice.

159

The guards knocked but did not wait for an answer before kicking the door of Beatral's lodge apart. The father and the son lay on narrow beds in the main room, a cold, grey hearth at its centre. Both were dead, and they displayed all the signs of advanced Bronzene. They had chosen not to seek medical attention.

The guards, wearing full face masks and isolated air supplies, overturned chests, tore up boards and wrenched doors off cupboards. They found nothing illicit. We moved to a shed behind the main house. It contained the tools one would expect of a labouring family, again nothing illicit. The guards turned back to the house, but I lingered. As they entered the back door I took a pair of heavy duty gloves from a nail and pushed them down my trousers.

A burial party was summoned; it landed before we left the premises. Time was those bodies would have been taken to the infirmary and dissected by our pathologist, but there was nothing more to learn from hacking through the layers of iron.

I asked Shenlee to scrape residue from the gloves and have it analysed. She came back with a result four hours later.

'Organic material, that is mud and crops, phosphate-nitrogen fertiliser... and Tellurium. High concentration. Very high. But I don't get it. Bronzene is a disease of iron. What's Tellurium got to do with it?'

In my mind the toxin hypothesis was proven. Tellurium. The victims were part of a trade or living with those who were involved in it. But the story was incomplete. I had no idea why such a trade had developed. What's more, I knew that Bowl-border dwellers, those living closest to Tellurium deposits, had never presented with symptoms like Bronzene. If the disease was a reaction to Tellurium, why now? I needed more information before going back to the King.

There were things going on in the kingdom that I did not understand. I needed information.

My contact at court was an outsider who knew all that there was to know about Lannert. Her knowledge was comprehensive precisely *because* she was an outsider; she had taught herself everything before taking up her position as the College of Dominions' ambassador to Lannert.

Lannert's history only extended back as far as 750 years, to when the first colonists arrived. Despite their successes in taming the environment and making the planet productive, the early period of the Lannert's history was dominated by strife – strife that was only resolved when a revolution displanted the original royal line and replaced it with a new one. The victory of King Patrolian, the first of the new line, was immortalised by a huge double statue cut from granite which overlooked the city's landing zone. His face was serene and handsome, the long features of our species accentuated by the sculptor. His vanquished rival for the throne, Flenta, faced him. A fraction shorter, but broader, his stocky limbs and short neck suggesting an uncultured philosophy. He was topped off by a mean mouth and narrowed, malevolent eyes. There was no doubt about it, as the histories explained in florid detail, Flenta's defeat had saved our futures from corruption. He had no children. His bloodline was cut the moment Patrolian's blade severed one of the main arteries in his neck. The present king, Mantel, paid homage at Patrolian's massive feet twice a year. The ceremony was long. The whole kingdom took a holiday, and watched on screens, or in person if they could make their way to the capital.

Although Lannert was a self-governing kingdom, wider policies that might affect it were developed by the College of Dominions. The College was based on the origin planet where its staff and buildings occupied the space of a small city. Its ambassadors, though, were not always welcome on the peripheral worlds, including Lannert. Back through the centuries several had disappeared, and it was supposed that their sand-scoured bones lay somewhere out there in the Bowl-border.

So, my contact Grace kept herself ahead of the multifarious and dangerous internal games of court by ensuring that she knew things before her opponents understood their significance. Moreover, she liked me. She enjoyed my irreverence towards the spoilt young king, who was no friend of hers. I requested that she come to the infirmary, being unable myself to visit the embassy. She took two days to reply, but agreed.

We talked on the roof, looking out across the city, the wall of the mountain behind us. It was dusk. Craft came and went from the landing areas that covered several of the foothills, all overlooked by the statues of Patrolian and his historic enemy. Grace, her black hair cut severely around a serious face that could crack into humour at any moment, commiserated with my situation and assured me that it had been reported back to the origin planet.

'Grace, I think Bronzene is caused by long term exposure to Tellurium.'

'*Tellurium?*' Her emphasis on the word assured me that she had heard of it. If she had heard of it, it must be important.

'The very word stunned you. What do you know?'

'Probably not enough to help you, Stephen. Have you told anyone else about this theory?'

'No one. One of my juniors probably knows.'

'Then he—'

'She.'

'Then she should be sent away. The King would rather see a quarter of the population succumb to Bronzene than risk having a link with Tellurium made public. And that's nothing compared to what he will do – and has already done – if he thought the cause were genetic. You are in an impossible situation, Stephen.'

The meaning of this didn't immediately sink in with me, and I concentrated on finding out what more Grace could tell me with regard to the Tellurium angle. 'What is Tellurium used for?' I asked her.

'I don't know exactly. But I do know that over the last five years it has been smuggled out of Lannert in small ingots, in a highly concentrated form. It's a metalloid – that's as technical as I get – and non-radioactive, so it doesn't set off any sensors.'

'So they're passing it as what… coal? Gold? Gems?'

'I don't know what they're passing it as. Perhaps they don't need to. Perhaps the customs and excise officers have been paid off. Like your king. I didn't say that, by the way. This is what I know. The skim is keeping him in monuments and new projects, his agro and export policies aren't enough to keep Lannert above the line. He's not secure Stephen. He won't let you reveal this element as the cause of Bronzene.'

'Then I can never leave.'

'Find a cure. That will solve the problem for you and for him.'

'The only cure is avoidance.'

'Not an option. The mining of it cannot be stopped now. What if they wear masks and suits?'

I considered.

'No. It's not happening in the mines. If those who live near the mines are not affected, it must be something to do with the concentration. The pure product. These people must have refined it in factories, or stored it in their houses, under the floor boards. Some of their relatives lived above it…'

'Until the collectors arrived and paid them. I see, Stephen. But it still doesn't…'

Grace stared, looking up at the mountain behind us, as though searching the scenery for a prompt.

'What?' I asked.

'We've been here before. Before your time, before mine. Tellurium I mean. It was discovered centuries ago. It was abandoned.'

'*What?*'

'It's in the dominion histories. I've read it. You must be aware.'

'I searched Tellurium in relation to this planet… and found next to nothing. Only its existence under the mountains.'

'There's more. It was mined at the time of the succession war. It was a source of wealth then, as it clearly is now. The records do not tell who or what received the cargo. But that element fuelled a great rivalry between the houses of Flenta and Patrolian. The trade was hidden even then, for fear that the origin planet would find out and suppress the new dominion. Not surprising then, that the records here on Lannert do not give much away.'

I looked out over my city and felt hatred for it, and for its personification, the King. A king I had been proud to serve, even if I had never grown to like him. I looked at the King's ancestor Patrolian, then across at Flenta the vanquished. His mean face, his narrowed eyes, his terse lips. And something about the distance, the angle, the amber light of dusk, turned the key and unlocked the mystery. Tellurium, the great tree, Bronzene, Patrolian, Flenta… all connected.

'Take me to him,' I demanded

'Who?' asked Grace.

'The King. Who else?'

'Stephen, so good to have you back!' Mantel pronounced with official bonhomie. He wore a dark blue robe with a four-weave silver border. 'I heard about your three genealogists, by the way. Out of my hands, but they had to pay for past crimes. Would you believe it, they had been selling titles. Like selling blood, if you ask me. You can't fiddle blood-lines, Stephen. What would become of us, stuck out here on the far side of the sector? We must have rules to…'

Perhaps he detected something dangerous in my poorly concealed smirk, perhaps the notion of 'doth protest too much' came to his own mind, but his smile faded and his words trailed off. After a moment's silence he changed tack.

'So, esteemed doctor, tell us. Why are my subjects dying?'

'Greed, sire.'

'A good start, Stephen! Dramatic. Continue.'

'The victims have been in close and sustained proximity to concentrated Tellurium.'

His breathing altered, first fast, then slow. I noticed as I am trained to count the breaths of my patients.

'Tellurium? The element that nearly tore our new world apart in the time of Patrolian and Flenta. What have you discovered, Stephen? Has it become poisonous?' His jocular expression was fixed and tense. The mask of guilt. What, I wondered, was his escape phrase? Some combination of words that, if uttered, would trigger the poised guards to assail me, to shut me up.

'The Tellurium is the same, Your Majesty. I have no knowledge of its role, its uses, its importance, its... rewards. I have not tried to discover those things. But I know that the victims of Bronzene have been poisoned by the particles it sheds. The element is breathed in, or absorbed through the skin, or ingested by those who prepare food and drink near its concentrated form. Once in the body it displaces iron from the blood cells and forces it out through the skin. Slowly, or quickly relative to many other types of poisoning, the iron accretes, forms a hard layer. The iron is not enough by itself – our bodies do not contain enough to form a full coating – but in combination with other natural substances, such as carbon, phosphate or calcium, it produces the hard, variegated shell that we have all seen. That is my answer.'

'We thank you, Stephen. Most here present know that the trade in Tellurium has grown from nothing over the past decade, despite all our efforts to suppress it.'

I looked at the intricately patterned tiles on the floor, sickened by his lies.

He continued, 'Yet... lay person as I am, forgive me, but Tellurium did not cause such an affliction many years ago when it was mined openly, traded in the streets, in those relatively lawless times. Surely your theory is disproved… by history. We know that Tellurium is not harmful.'

'*We* have changed, Your Highness.'

'In what way?' His tone was uncertain; it lacked the confidence of one who had usually been told the answer to his questions in private before the answer was given in public. And here, now, was very public indeed.

'We have changed. It is called the Founder Effect. Imagine an unknown inherited disease carried by just 1 in 1000 people. Take ten random people, screen them for known disease and send them off to form a colony. Now imagine that one of those ten *carries the gene for the disease*. Within the colony the frequency will now be 1 in 10, a hundred times more common than in the origin population. Generations to come will have a hugely increased chance of suffering the disease. Imagine the disease is dominant rather than recessive. Over time a great number will be afflicted. This is what I think has happened.'

Verrilian stooped to whisper something. The King nodded. I didn't know how much he knew or suspected – if anything. Had the great tree of the genealogists been partially wiped before I came to see it? Was he simply paranoid?

'With respect Stephen… I am confused. Is Bronzene a genetic disease or a form of poisoning? It can't be both, surely.'

'I thought the same, sire, but it is. Our ability to cope with Tellurium depends on an enzyme. The enzyme binds Tellurium to chloride, forming a harmless salt that is excreted in the urine. The genetic defect responsible for Bronzene causes ultra-low levels of that enzyme. Those with the mutation remain well until exposed to Tellurium. Once exposed, the toxic effects come on rapidly. In fact, there is an exponential effect. One tellurium atom can displace 100,000 iron atoms. The accumulation of iron on the skin is unstoppable.'

'But…' – his confusion was, I was now sure, genuine – 'this is a *new* condition. If our ancestors carried this… defect… why did they not show the signs?'

'Over many generations the influence of a genetic defect can grow. The number of errors in the gene can increase. I believe that is what has been happening here. Penetrance has increased and has coincided with a renewed trade in Tellurium.'

'Stephen, I don't pretend to understand it all, but I think I believe you.' He looked around, took in the nods and the murmurs of assent. 'Yes, we believe you. But what do we do?'

'Ban the trade in Tellurium.'

'Ah. Ah. That is not so easy.'

'You have the power to do so, Your Majesty.' Now I was out of line. But he did not have me arrested. He sensed, I think, that there was more to come.

'That I do, Stephen. And as physician to your king, and therefore to my people, I respect your conviction and can overlook your insolence. But I have to be mindful of larger concerns. Tell me, your best estimate… how many of our fellow men and women may fall prey to this disease if Tellurium continues to be mined?'

'It depends on the cumulative exposure. Perhaps… thirty percent.'

'And when they have passed on, those who have inherited the bad genes… what of those who are left behind?'

'They will be safe.' I knew now what he was suggesting. A passive eugenics programme. A laissez-faire attitude that would result in the vulnerable being culled. Any hesitancy or cowardice that I had felt now fell away.

'Your Majesty... I know why your people are suffering.'

'You have told us. Thank you.'

Too late, sire, to shut me down. I have the attention of the whole court. They don't yet know what I know... and what, deep down, you know too.

'No, sire, please listen. I understand how the mutated gene propagated through our population. To prove my theory I had to identify the source, the prime carrier.'

'I'm not sure we—'

But I talked over him. 'The disease is not new, you see. It manifested itself during the war of succession.'

'How?' His question seemed genuine. He did not know. He wanted to know.

'Flenta. He was the first victim. He was greatly exposed keeping a secret hoard of Tellurium. The wealth he accumulated created the conditions for war, and he fought the final battle with your ancestor Patrolian while in the grip of it. It gave him strength, strangely, or perhaps he was given drugs to boost his strength on the eve of battle. But his face was already set, his features fixed... look at the statue out there, look at the face, the slit-like mouth, the lightless eyes... he died of Bronzene... the death blow did not penetrate his self-grown armour... he suffocated on the field. That is why he became legend. He was impervious to the sword blow. And his clay death mask, on which the statue's face is based, reflects that obduracy. He carried the mutation. He was the first, the only... and it killed him.'

169

'Then how, why, do we see it now, centuries later? His line was terminated.'

'Because before he died he conceived a child... with the wife of Patrolian... with the Queen... with your... your ancestor.'

He was stunned. Yet he knew it to be true. I continued, knowing that my words – laced with hate, superfluous perhaps – could result only in a death sentence. 'The royal line are the children of Flenta. My genealogists were approaching the same conclusion, having been given the crucial genetic data from the first 500 victims... but their work was cut short, as you know. The nobility are all the children of Flenta. Even you, dear King, a descendant of the first bastard, are carrying the mutation that—'

That was enough. Guards surrounded me, knocked me down, pressed my face to the floor, held my neck...

Until – with commotion all around me – I opened my eyes to see different guards in unfamiliar livery, Imperial not Dominian, not seen on this planet for a century or more... with Grace, tall, confident, giving orders, pointing this way and that. Then strong men with hard hands under my shoulders, carrying me away, to the landing zone. I looked up at the great statues, at Flenta's too-square chin, his narrow mouth, his flared nostrils, immobile features stilled by illness... before the ship into which I was bundled accelerated away from Lannert. I tried to get up from the reclining position into which the Imperial guards had put me, but Grace placed her hand on my forehead and dipped her face into view, filling my vision.

'No Stephen, you're hurt. Don't move. You are needed, on the origin planet. Your testimony. It has been decided it's time to change the regime. Don't worry. Don't worry.'

I feared for all those who had been connected to me on Lannert. I thought of Shenlee, my closest associate.

'The resident in the hospital, she's in danger…'

'No Stephen.' Grace moved to one side, and in the corner of the ship's bay I saw Shenlee, her anxious expression, those delicate hands.

'They thought of everything, Dr Iss… Stephen. Don't worry. Rest. Soon, Bronzene will exist only in the textbooks.'

WAKE UP TO YOURSELF

Aviva Treger

R ight now, I'm sitting in a queue about to have my memories erased, and soon they'll be lost forever. Such things are inevitable, I suppose, or so they tell me; but in these last few minutes, while I still can, I want to recall the day I first saw her, before it's all gone; and when it's all gone, as a common courtesy, maybe for the time being, you could remember it for me, on my behalf – at least until the moment comes when you have your memories erased too.

The day I first saw her she was slumped by the window in the waiting room, her eyes half-closed, and at first I thought she was squinting in the sun's harsh glare – January was incredibly hot that year; but after I'd checked my notes, I realised she'd probably just fallen asleep. When I next looked she was blinking, peering down at the garden, at its flock of raucous macaws in the banana trees, then into the distance at the livestock grazing on the rooftop farms over Sussex. She stirred when her name was called, and I watched her struggle to rise, then walk with a trace of a limp towards me. I smiled a warm 'Hello', because appearing to be friendly to patients was an important part of my job then, even though they often didn't notice. She wore an empty expression as I guided

172

her to the doctor's office and, from behind the white desk, as the door opened, I saw Dr Alecto glance up askance, and in a sharp tone of voice address her and say, 'You again. What is it now, Theia? What's the matter with you today?'

Afterwards, I lead her back to the entrance of The Clinic, discussing what the doctor had prescribed – how it uploaded, how it interfaced and how to liaise with me should she have any issues. 'I'm the Medical Technician assigned to you,' I said, showing my ID and smiling. 'I'll be monitoring your progress throughout the treatment, mainly via telepresence, so please don't hesitate to chat to me at any time, about anything.' She yawned in response, impassive, gawping into empty space as if I wasn't there, then stumbled off into the stifling afternoon without even saying goodbye.

I know she went straight home because, as I said, I was monitoring her. She ate, showered and went to bed early, attaching the device from the doctor in the way I'd shown, and within a short time, according to my remote observation feed, she was responding well to it. Theia fell asleep, and soon after the programme began to run. A peaceful dream gradually sharpened into focus, revealing the fresh colours of an alpine landscape with a lush flowering meadow and a turquoise stream set against the backdrop of a crisp flawless day. I saw the images unfold in the dream as she did. I saw the whirling pairs of butterflies above the wild lavender and the shimmering rainbow on the horizon. I heard the sweet trill of songbirds and an omniscient voice, reassuring and calm, guiding the words of a sleep meditation. As she relaxed further, the scenery drifted, then gently faded away, transforming into the dreamless oblivion of deepest sleep.

In the morning, Theia's vital signs all recorded as healthy. She'd slept without disturbance the whole night through, which was encouraging, although the treatment is nearly always effective the first time. I noted she had a good appetite for breakfast, eating a bowl of seaweed flakes and a whole moonfruit, and then she left for her job in centenarian care management. It was late afternoon when I received a call from her, whilst I was off duty. On the screen, she looked revitalised with much more animation in her face than yesterday, but she seemed agitated. I smiled and said, 'How are you?' but she ignored that. Instead, she questioned me about the side-effects of her prescribed therapy, so I reeled off the list, urging her to elaborate the reason for her query, but she just tutted and said, 'I really hate having to deal with you.'

There was a silence, so I thought it best to fill it by apologising for any perceived flaw regarding my empathy and explain that I'd only been working with civilians for a short time. Again, I bid her to please continue, and this time she did. Theia said she'd been seeing things, images in reflective surfaces or in the corner of her eye that mirrored the scenery from the dream but with a macabre, frightening quality imbued and, in some instances, the landscape had appeared to be on fire. 'And that voice,' she said, 'that voice from the dream, again and again. I've been hearing that voice all day.' I asked what it had said, but she wouldn't answer.

As we spoke, I searched through my notes on the inducing of deep sleep via brain stimulation, but I could find no reference to waking hallucinations as a side-effect; so, weighing the pros and cons, I decided to advise that the visions would probably wear off once a normal sleep cycle had been established and that we should continue the treatment a little longer.

With a huff of irritation, she agreed to this – maybe just to get rid of me; so I said goodbye and left her alone. But I remained watching, and I know how she spent the evening, what she ate, when she bathed, what she read, what she wore, and I recorded when she lay down that night. And as she turned over and surrendered to sleep, the dreamscape activated again, slowly metamorphosing into view. This time, I'd chosen a forest scene for her, a clearing with shafts of mellow sunlight and ancient moss-covered trees. I thought she might like the fragrant pine needles crunching underfoot and the sound of a woodpecker echoing from deep inside the copse and the inquisitive red squirrels, extinct now of course, foraging amongst the bluebells.

Theia was responding well to the sensory stimuli until the voice-over script began, intoning a loop of hypnotic words intended to aid a soothing descent into rest. It was at this juncture that I noticed her heartbeat and pulse rate start to speed up, so I was just about to mute the voice in the programme when something odd happened in the dream that, in all my years of monitoring people during induced sleep sessions, I've never seen before.

A seemingly random character appeared. A young man with a mass of curly dark hair stepped out of the trees. He was speaking the words of the voice-over script and, with abruptness, mid-sentence, he stopped. He remained motionless, as if waiting, and he wore a curious curving smile as though he was aware of an audience. Then, as he stood there, at the corner of his mouth I noticed a trickle of blood begin to ooze and rivulet downwards, dripping onto his white clothes. A fresh wound deepened in colour near to his temple and started to seep blood, spattering flecks of crimson across his face, across that strange relentless lingering grin.

At that instant, my attention jolted back to Theia because she gulped for breath in her sleep and was trying to speak, trying to move. I aborted the dream sequence at once, and I know from her perspective the dream world would have warped, buckling into twisted shadow, and she would have suffered the eerie sensation of falling out of it, falling into a dark fog, engulfed by the ear-splitting hiss and shriek of white noise. It took some time for her to regain consciousness, and when she finally did she woke up coughing and spluttering, shaking and crying, her skin goose-pimpled with cold. In the gloom of her bedroom, again and again, she refused to answer me when I tried to console her.

I wondered what to do. I debated whether to go there in person, but decided against it since she'd clearly taken a dislike to me and would hardly feel comforted by my presence. So, instead, I watched her with a keen vigilance all night. She didn't try to sleep again, and when dawn spread across the sky she got dressed and went out. She walked for an hour in the tropical gardens, which were visible on surveillance cameras, so I could follow her; then she came here to The Clinic, as I thought she might, intent on speaking to Dr Alecto before the day's appointments began. I saw her arguing with the automated receptionist on the front desk, and I tried to intervene because those stupid machines have an appalling lack of rapport with patients, but Theia told me to go to hell, that she only wanted to talk to the doctor and would wait however long it took. I tried not to take this personally; I really did understand her frustration, so I returned to my duties.

After a while, I saw her sneak up the corridor when the mechanicals weren't looking and loiter around the doctor's office. She finally entered unannounced when someone came out and, through the doorway, I saw Dr Alecto grimace at the intrusion, glowering with his usual misanthropy; but he relented and the door closed on them both. Obviously I shouldn't eavesdrop on private conversations, but it's easy to do so in my line of work, and I wanted to know what was discussed. Mainly it was the hallucinations and the nightmare, but I also heard Theia say, 'That Technician is spying on my every move. It really gives me the creeps,' which was embarrassing, but I put it down to exhaustion on her part, because in a ragged, pitiful voice she then said, 'I'm so tired. I think I'd rather die than always be this tired.'

There was a silence. Then Dr Alecto cleared his throat and replied. 'I read your medical notes with interest,' he said. 'You had a brain injury, didn't you? In view of that, perhaps I shouldn't have prescribed this kind of therapy for a sleep disorder.' There was another silence. Then he added, 'But maybe you deserve everything you get.'

I heard Theia's reel of surprise. She started to form a response, but the doctor continued talking nonetheless. 'You killed someone,' he said with matter-of-fact smugness. 'I read the report. "Asleep at the wheel" it said. What a quaint, archaic term that is these days. How did you get access to an antique car, anyway?' She didn't answer, and in the ensuing pause I imagined he subjected her to a scathing glare. He then said, 'I suppose you still can't remember anything?'

Theia muttered a reply. 'No,' she said, 'I... I have no memory at all of that night.' Her breathing was fraught, and it pained me to hear her in distress – it pained me to the core. I'm amazed at the inhumanity of the doctors in this clinic, who think they can behave without any consideration for people's feelings, just because there are so few real doctors around these days. I deliberated whether I should feign an excuse to enter the room, but then I heard Dr Alecto sigh loudly and say, 'Well, he's dead now, your unlucky passenger, and if you see him in your dreams, why not apologise for killing him when he next turns up?' He dispensed a hollow bark of a laugh and then said, 'Continue the treatment or don't. It's up to you.'

I was hovering outside the door when Theia burst from the room; she rushed off, then tripped over whilst leaving the building. A droid zoomed towards her to offer assistance, but I swatted it aside with a kick, helping her up myself. I thought she might tell me to go away again, but instead she grasped my arm and gazed at me with a tragic intensity, and for the first time she looked me right in the eye. 'I want to go back,' she said, 'back to that dream – and speak to him. Can I even do that?'

I thought about her question. 'Yes and no,' I said, rattling off the reasons why we never advise the use of lucid dreaming programmes as they're very different from therapeutic dreams and can have unpredictable, even potentially dangerous side-effects if used without care. But she pleaded with me, still holding my arm, and in view of the cruelty the doctor had just shown, I felt duty bound to assist her. So that evening, I acquired some lucid dreaming software. We talked for a while first – I made it clear to her I'd have to withdraw her from any scenario if she became overwrought – then she retired to bed, and I watched her remotely as before.

When she was asleep, bit by bit the lucid dreamscape materialised, at first a charcoal grey blur, but then it cleared into a starless night-time scene, dank and murky with a crescent moon above and a soft drizzling rain. We were at a dimly lit crossroads in the middle of an empty road. Out of the gloaming, I saw the wreckage of a battered dented vehicle, old-fashioned and obsolete, and nearby another piece of debris was smouldering, still with embers of flame. Theia reached out towards the car, opening its passenger door and, sharing her viewpoint, what I could see inside was a shadowy mass of a body, a young man with curly hair. He was slumped in the seat unmoving, his pale face, with that upwardly curving mouth, turned towards the faint light. But then he seemed to rouse; he opened his dark eyes and he blinked.

Then something unexpected happened – my observation feed went dead. I tried again and again to re-establish it, because I couldn't allow her to continue without supervision. After several attempts, I decided to manually withdraw Theia from the dream by hacking into her domestic service butler and ordering it to help me, but it was then that I realised she wasn't actually present anymore. She wasn't in bed, asleep or awake; she wasn't in the bathroom; she wasn't anywhere at home. I patched into the security cameras in her building, on her street, and searched, but I couldn't find where she'd gone. I eventually located her by microchip ID tracker; she was at an isolated site on the edge of the city at a crossroads, and because my readings suggested she was unconscious, I alerted an emergency team to reach her faster than I could.

They brought her back to The Clinic with bloodied feet and torn flimsy pyjamas, apparently having sleepwalked into the night under the influence of an induced trance. I knew I'd be in big trouble now, firstly for facilitating her actions and not supervising them properly, but secondly for involving myself in her experience rather than dispassionately observing it. But I was astonished to find I didn't care; I only cared about Theia – about her needs, her wishes, her dreams and that she was safe. I stayed there by her bedside, watching, until she was fully awake.

It was Dr Erebus who arrived to attend her. I usually avoid him, as he's prejudiced and bigoted towards staff like me, staff who originally trained for combat in war zones; but I remained present whilst he spoke to Theia, discussing her past – the car crash, the night terrors and the post-traumatic stress. 'Dr Alecto should've mentioned the latest option,' said Dr Erebus. 'Amnesia surgery. Soon, everyone will want it done. You could have all memories of the accident, and the people connected to it, both conscious and subconscious, permanently removed. Then you could live in blissful indifference with all the worries of life blotted out.'

As Theia contemplated this solution, I saw her face crumple; I saw her eyes flinch, then brim with tears, and even though it could've lost me my job, I felt compelled to shield her. So, I blurted out that she was in no fit state to be making such decisions now, that she was overwrought, vulnerable and needed quality rest and why couldn't he have the sensitivity to see that.

I thought he'd be annoyed by my outburst but, instead, Dr Erebus guffawed to himself with oafish disdain. 'It never ceases to amaze me,' he said, 'how much

WAKE UP TO YOURSELF

you ex-military types think you're actually a comfort to your patients. You've killed thousands – you're the stuff of nightmares.' He sniggered again as I reached out for Theia's delicate hand, holding it with tenderness between both of mine as she wept. And, in a tone of ugly, cutting sarcasm, as he left the room he said, 'What do you know about anything, anyway? Your thoughts don't count – you'll forget them when you're next brainwashed. You're under orders to care or to kill, and to do your duty, but you're not real. You're only a convenience, only a tool – wake up to yourself. You're just a heartless robot.'

THE SPACEWALK

Colette Bennett

Y *ou're too old to be out here.*

Elena Amano took a deep breath as she stood before the vast void of space at the portal on her right and tried to steady herself. 55 was not too old. Not too old to go on a trip to the moon, not too old to go on a spacewalk (which, admittedly, was part of the tour and sort of a spacewalk-lite with a guide). Sena had been 50 when he'd come up here for his first Mars assignment.

First… and last.

"We're going to get into our suits now, everyone," said a handsome young man with a decidedly Alec Baldwin-circa-*Beetlejuice* look, interrupting her reverie. "If you grew up watching NASA broadcasts, you're probably wondering where the EMUs are – what you know as the puffy white suits. While they hold a significant place in our history, things have changed quite a bit since 2037! The new EMU is 89 percent thinner and lighter…"

A stubby blonde woman wearing a pink cardigan was looking at their host with an expression of distinct hunger. The worn-looking man she presumed to be the husband was trying not to notice this as the young man continued to extol all the benefits of the spacesuits.

She personally couldn't care less about how they'd changed, or how much lighter they were. She wasn't here to have the cutting edge version of the spacewalk experience. All she really cared about was being able to see the thing that she had drawn with painstaking detail over and over again in her mind, to give it some solidity, to force her thoughts to stop filling in the details of what may or may not have happened.

She wanted to see where Sena had gone.

"...the Primary Life Support Subsystem, PLSS for short, is also much lighter. In fact, when astronaut Russell Schweickart wore it during the Apollo 9 mission, his PLSS weighed 84 pounds! In Earth weight, that is." A polite chuckle from the audience. "It actually only weighed 14 pounds on the Moon. Thanks to exhaustive technological developments, now it only weighs seven..."

Sena wore the heavy kind.

He'd stopped talking about his job as he'd gotten older. She supposed it would have been hard to relate, even though she did try to listen even when it all sounded like gobbleygook. Before the kids were grown, they used to ask tons of questions. She remembered how Sena's face lit up when he told them the story of the first time he went into orbit. But as they grew into teenagers, they stopped asking and he stopped talking. Not just to them, but to her, too.

"...the EVA gloves haven't changed. That's because your fingers are the part of the body that gets coldest in space, so they need extra protection! But hang onto your manicure, because the gloves are hard on your fingernails..."

Pink Cardigan tittered at this, bringing Elena back to the moment. She suppressed a smile as she noticed the husband looking at his wife with a mixture of disdain and jealousy.

Sena never looked at me like that.

When Sena was called to Mars back in '41, the kids had long moved out. The two of them traveled their own orbits in the old cottage house, briefly passing by one another from time to time. Not roommates, not partners. Something had been lost along the way. She wasn't sure if it was raising the kids, or not being able to adjust to life without that job to do. 28 years of marriage was a long time, and the rules for how to get it right seemed to swim away every time she thought she got close. No one had told her how hard it could be when she was a new bride, or any time before. No one dared.

Three days before her 54th birthday, the call came. He'd vanished during a routine spacewalk, his radio communication cut off as cleanly as a sharp knife parting ripe fruit. The crew had searched for him but found no traces except for the tool kit he brought with him to repair a small satellite, which they found tethered to the ship outside of the worksite.

Despite the strange distance that seemed to have invaded their marriage, she loved her husband dearly. And even though she had no way to understand what had happened, she kept trying. It was as if some part of her brain just refused to give up without an answer. Which was unfortunate, since there were no answers to be found.

"This place we live in, this is only a tiny part of the universe," Sena had said to her one misty winter morning on the front porch when she was still pregnant with their first son. She had just poured tea for them both, something they enjoyed together regularly over the many years of their marriage.

"Five percent, right?"

"Yep. There's so much mystery up there that we can't begin to grasp. And yet we keep going up and trying. 68 percent of the universe is dark energy – and we don't even know what purpose that serves. Galaxies continue to pull apart at a faster and faster rate. And somehow all this has something to do with us. I'm sure of it."

She finished her cup and he stood up, gathering it to refill along with his own.

"You know, Elena, call me crazy, but I think it's a part of us."

"The dark energy?"

"ALL energy." Sena motioned at the sky. "Every plant, every animal, every human. I promise you that if you were up there with me, you'd feel it too. It's all familiar. We never really lose anyone, anything. It's all in there."

She hadn't understood. But she'd nodded anyway, not in understanding but at the bright fire in his eyes as he'd said it, recognizing how resonant those words were for him, how real. And now, recalling that moment decades later, she nodded again. It seemed possible to her that he was still out here, his spirit granulated into a billion tiny orbits, as he was inside her heart. He was there, so why not here?

When she'd seen the advertisements seeking civilian recruits for a year-long mission to Mars, she didn't hesitate. She didn't tell the children – they spoke very little these days. She cleaned out the long-untouched savings account she shared with Sena, packed a bag, and locked her front door.

She didn't feel sad leaving. She was going to meet her husband.

They had to wear the suits for three hours before leaving the ship – that much had not changed. Pressurized and filled with oxygen, they made it possible for humans to tolerate the harsh environment outside the ship. As she waited, Elena thought of each step in the preparation process as something Sena had experienced hundreds of times. How had he felt when he put on the spacesuit? Did it grow matter-of-fact after so many times? Had he ever felt afraid?

"Alright, ladies and gentlemen."

Young Buck (as Elena had named him in her head) appeared in the doorway to the hold, where many others were reading their visual displays to pass the time. Elena hadn't been reading anything; her thoughts were too full. She looked up at the sound of the cheery voice, fear crystallizing in her heart. But beneath it, she sensed the flow of a steady river: determination.

She stood up.

"Finally, we're ready. We'll send two at a time, in order of last name. Each person will spend 15 minutes on the spacewalk before we bring you back in. Should you want to come back sooner, radio and let us know. And please observe the regulations that were outlined in the agreements you signed this morning."

Shuffles and nods. Elena noticed an elderly man across from her putting on his gloves as he muttered something to himself.

"OK, first group: Amano and Andrews please."

She stepped forward. At first she thought Andrews had flown the coop, but eventually a young dark-haired woman who looked about 25 came to stand beside her. They nodded and smiled at one another.

"Wait, I'm Andrews," said the elderly man that Elena had noticed a moment before. He hobbled up, looking as if he was in no condition to stand without help, much less take a spacewalk.

"I am too," the young woman said.

Young Buck looked at both kindly, never breaking a sweat.

"This has happened before! When it does, we go by first name order. What are your first names?"

"Bethany," the young woman said, as the old man said "Benton."

Young Buck laughed cannily. "Close one! Alright Bethany, please wait for round two. Sorry for the confusion."

Looking peeved, Bethany returned to her seat. Mr. Benton slowly made his way beside Elena, his mouth kinked as a twist-tie.

"Follow me," Young Buck said with confidence.

After explaining the importance of the steel tethers that held them to the ship and checking their suits and helmets to make sure everything was in place, Elena and Mr. Benton were led to the airlock.

"Remember, in 15 minutes we'll bring you back in. Don't panic when you feel the tether being pulled – that will be us reeling you back."

Watching Young Buck explain the system – the steel tether to hold the astronaut to the ship and the SAFER unit, which worked like a jetpack – it made less sense than ever to Elena how Sena had vanished. How had these things not saved his life? Why was no one there to reel him back? She'd had no one to ask these questions, and it made her angry.

"Excuse me," she said to Young Buck, and he turned his full Plastic n' Pleasant smile on her as if to say, yes, how may I serve you today?

Not knowing what she was going to say before she said it, she felt the words tumble out of the pain in her guts.

"How possible is it for either of these safety precautions to malfunction?"

"Oh, hardly. In fact, we've only had three incidents with them in the history of NASA's spacewalks, and as you likely know that's a 78 year timespan."

"Yes, I know," she heard herself saying, as if there was a ventriloquist in the room pantomiming her voice. "My husband was one of them."

Young Buck visibly lost his composure, the edge of his mask slipping. But he quickly reassembled himself, and she watched as the broad smile melted into an appropriate expression of troubled care.

"I am SO sorry to hear that, Mrs. Amano. If there's anything I can do to make this experience easier on you, please let me know."

There isn't.

As he turned away to do whatever final preparations were left, she felt something touch her glove. Looking up, she saw that Mr. Andrews was clasping it between his own. His face had transformed from testy to something that took her by surprise: warmth, infinite kindness. He was looking her directly in the eyes.

"I lost my wife too," he said, still watching her face. "If you'd like, we should talk after the spacewalk. I have a few things to share that may help you."

Elena nodded, unable to speak around the lump that had risen in her throat. She felt like she was going to cry, not just cry but wail, scream, vomit up some horrible demon of pain she was unable to control but would spew out of her anyway.

"Call me Benton," he said, and then seeming to sense her struggle, nodded and turned away to leave her be.

The airlock door opened.

Beyond the round metal portal, the first thing she saw was stars. Billions of them, more than she had ever seen even on the clearest stargazing nights of her life. They enclosed her like a cloak. Blackness, forever blackness.

The silence was absolute and beautiful. A sense of complete calm washed over her, drenching her fear and anxiety. If only to find this place again when her heart was hurting! It felt like pure relief, a place where the voices in her head turned off. Nothing they could say could have much precedence over this.

"Alright astronauts, you're on a spacewalk! How do you feel?"

Young Buck on the radio, chipper as ever. Mr. Andrews (*Benton*, her brain whispered) was radioing back to him, but she didn't reply until he prompted her a second time.

"Mrs. Amano? You OK?"

She fumbled until she found her call button.

"Yes."

"Good! Let us know if you have any questions out there."

She barely heard him. As her tether was let out the vision of the blackness before her became infinite, a length of velvet folded over and over. She sensed its

189

depth, but found she was unable to grasp it with her tiny mind. Too big. It came to her that it was a wonder Sena had ever come home. How could anyone bear to leave this peace? This silence?

It's all familiar. We never really lose anyone, anything. It's all in there.

Was it familiar? At first it seemed like the most unfamiliar thing she had ever experienced. Nothing on Earth could compare to it. She could see Earth, in fact, off to her left over a smaller celestial body. Its moon. She raised her gloved hand and covered it with a single finger, blotting it out of existence.

We are that small. We really are.

She closed her eyes for a moment and felt it: the smallness, the inconsequential nature of her being. Felt how every tragedy in her life, even Sena's death, was simply a blip in the universe. And something inside her that was clenched like a fist softened and unfurled. As tiny as everything was in comparison to this, it also all intertwined. She saw this with crystal clarity. Just like a pond that rippled with every movement, this space-time was aware of absolutely everything.

"He was right," Elena breathed in her helmet as warm tears started to course down her cheeks. "God, he was right."

Her body trembled with grief, but it was interrupted by another voice in her head, one she didn't recognize.

You don't have long.

A lurch of despair. She couldn't stay here long. And if he was here, she had something she needed to say. Needed for him to hear.

Her finger went to her call button, checking to make sure it was off. When she was satisfied that it was, she took a deep breath through her nostrils, then opened her eyes. She imagined the blackness of her vision flowing through her, making up her lungs, her guts. Stars knitting her bones into the shapes of legs, arms, a strong neck.

Sena. I'm here.

"Ten minutes left, folks," Young Buck announced brightly. If she could have punched his voice, she would have. Instead, she ignored it and focused on the husband she remembered, his soft brown eyes, the fleshiness of his smile. Her next inhale brought a choked sob.

I wish we could share tea again.

Some of the helmet's visor fogged, making it harder for her to see. In her mind's eye she saw steam rising off the surface of her old stoneware teacup, the one with the bluish glaze. The careful way he carried the saucer in one palm and looped a finger through the handle with the other hand. His kind eyes.

How she felt safe with him. Safe.

Where did you go? How could you leave?

She cast these thoughts furiously out into the void, anger unfurling from the emotions that were vulnerable only moments before. Her chest burned, a galaxy home to a boiling planet of fire. She'd felt pain there before, but not this. She felt a terrible persistence blooming, along with an agony so deep it terrified her, an ocean that she could dive for years and never find the floor of. Was this thing what she carried inside her every day? This horrible thing?

"Elena, Benton, you both doing OK? We have five more minutes."

It took every ounce of resolve in her body to respond to the call, but she knew she had to or she'd lose the little time she had.

"I'm OK."

"Me too." Benton, sounding a little wobbly despite his affirmation.

As it went silent again it dawned on her: it was almost over.

All the money she had spent, the life she had left behind, for this fifteen minutes. It was madness to be out here, utter stupidity. Her husband was not out here in the cold void of space, holding dear to some otherworldly transmission from an errant galaxy. He was dead.

The tears that blurred her vision were not sadness, but shame. She was old. She was a fool. She never should have come. She could be at home enjoying the house Sena had left behind, getting halfhearted calls from her kids a few times a year, baking for one in their roomy kitchen. It was both normal and awful. But it was also the only life she had.

She was fumbling for her call button angrily, to ask to be brought back in early, when a single word came into her consciousness, a completely foreign object.

Elena gasped. Each letter passed through her one at a time scrolling like a digital marquee from left to right, a long whisper from a source unknown. It took the pain in her heart with it, a great wind blowing through a tunnel. It gathered the moss from the walls, the dirt left behind by the hurried paws of animals. It wiped everything clean.

E   L   E   N   A

Golden, she thought disjointedly. *The letters are golden.*

There was no sound and no voice, but even without those things she knew.

"Sena," she whispered huskily, sobbing.

After they were back inside the ship, Young Buck gave them time to decompress after taking off their spacesuits. Elena found herself in a little room no bigger than a broom closet with a styrofoam cup of chamomile tea in hand. She only looked up when she felt a blanket settling around her shoulders and saw Benton had brought it.

"Thank you," she murmured, pulling it closer with her free hand.

He sat down across from her and smiled kindly. For a while, the silence between them was not uncomfortable at all. Two humans, side by side, still in the flow of their dovetailing lives.

Benton sipped at his own cup, and the moments wandered by.

"Did you talk to him?"

Elena stared at him with eyes that had grown painfully large. She opened her mouth to reply and choked out a sob, clapping a hand to her mouth in embarrassment immediately. But Benton's expression never changed.

He laid a warm hand on her shoulder.

"They're all there. My wife is too. I feel her all the time." He chuckled. "I don't believe in God or Heaven, even though Regina did. She knew there was more, but I was never convinced. Not until she had passed on, anyway."

Elena let this information sink in as she wiped her eyes with her fingertips.

"Do you... talk to her?"

"She talks to me." His smile grew softer, and for a moment she could see ages of love in it, decades more shared teas and breakfasts than she and Sena had time to know.

"Not with words, exactly. Sometimes it's a feeling or the way the air changes in a room. Every once in a while she sends me letters – not the written kind. It's hard to explain."

Elena inhaled shakily and started to cry again, sobs of ancient, familiar pain. She felt Benton take her styrofoam cup from her hand and she was glad. She buried her face in both hands and wept so hard that saliva fell from her contorted mouth in rivulets. Dimly, she felt the big hand on her shoulder patting her gently.

When her sobs started to calm, Benton said, "Do you know what an Ouroboros is?"

"Y-y-yes. The snake that eats its tail," she said, sounding cracked and terrible and not caring.

"Correct. Or, as some gnostics believe, a symbol of an infinite cycle of nature. Creation leads to destruction, life leads to death. There's centuries of speculation about all the variances of its meaning. But we can learn everything we need to learn by simply looking at it."

Elena shook her head, not comprehending what he was trying to say.

"The circle," he said, eyes lit with a confident spark. "Everything is connected. Made of the same stuff. I miss my wife, but I know she's only gone in one way. And it's OK to miss the way I knew her."

"I miss him," she said with a quavering voice. "But I only know one way to feel it. It feels like drowning every single day."

He nodded knowingly.

"Maybe now that you've spoken to him… things might change."

Elena couldn't reply. There were no words. She sat side by side with the old man, she wrapped in her blanket, him sipping at his coffee as steam curled up into his eyebrows. The silence returned. And in it, Elena realized, there was much more than she had ever heard before.

One year later

"Mrs. Amano! I think you dropped something!"

Elena looked up, the shade of her sun hat's brim making it hard for her to see. Ivan, the neighbor's boy, was running in her direction. As he drew closer to the fence, his crooked smile struck her with a wonderful charm. Only boys waiting for the tooth fairy looked like that.

Puffing, he skidded to a stop at the fence and held out three brilliant yellow daffodils in a plastic planter.

"Oh, I must have dropped that when I carried them from the car," Elena said, laying her trowel down on the window box. "I'm so glad you found it."

"I did!" The toothy smile bloomed again. Ivan had actually showed up more and more these days, as he was a latch key kid and often saw her gardening when he came home from school. He was eight, skinny as a rail, and sometimes came to her fence with sad eyes. Elena was quite familiar with that look from her bathroom mirror – but it had been some time since she'd seen it.

"Thank you so much. Do you want to help me plant? I can make you lunch after, if you'd like."

"Yeah!" There were no sad eyes now. "I have to clean my room first, but I'll hurry. I'll be there soon!"

She watched him run to his door, all gangly arms and legs. She knew he'd be back soon with lots of chatter, which always made her day all the brighter.

It'd taken a while after she'd come home to process what she'd experienced up there. Luckily, she'd had Benton's help, who she was now lucky enough to call a friend. He lived a three hour drive away, up in Washington, but they chatted a lot by phone, and he visited often. That chat after the spacewalk was the first of many. And these days, they cried less and laughed more.

He was actually due for a visit today, and as it was Friday he might stay the night in the guest room, as he often did now, rather than driving back late. Elena was looking forward to his visit.

She hollowed out a new spot in the dirt in the window box for the daffodil Ivan had brought. There were peonies and snapdragons in this one, and she had planned to put the daffodils in their own box. However, now that she stood here with them, it seemed just right that she add them to this box.

Daffodils, as she learned when she started poring over books about gardening, meant joy and happiness. That much was obvious from looking at their sunny yellow faces. It was also regarded as a sign of rebirth and eternal life. When she'd learned this, the vivid color of the flower took on a whole new meaning for her. She remembered her spacewalk when she looked at them, and hearing her own name in that great vast place. And she'd come to know that Sena had been right.

"Benton is coming to visit today," she murmured to the flowers as she tucked them into the hole she'd dug. "I think you'd like him. He's kind, just like you were."

Her eyes fell on the bright orange petals, the rumpled corona protecting its precious pistil. And somewhere in that brilliant color, she felt a flicker of her husband's spirit.

"I love you so," she said, smiling gently at the flower as she patted dirt around its stem. "I see you."

The sound of Benton's Tesla humming up the drive brought her out of her reverie. She turned to see him closing the passenger door and waving, and she returned it as she tucked her trowel into her apron pocket and went to meet him at the door.

"The drive feels shorter and shorter these days," he said, his eyes crinkling as he grinned. "I brought us some pastries from the new shop that opened near the house. You're going to love them!"

"I'll make us coffee," she said, smiling.

ASK MY SISTER

Melaina Barnes

G avin knew he was being watched from his ship and he knew his hesitation would be judged as weakness. But, oh, Nerida. Every nerve in his body told him to be still. To truly look at her.

Nerida's rusted cables of hair lifted and fell like waving reeds. Her polished red eyes reflected the vastness of space, and her sound – that thrum and drone – licked every fold of his brain.

When he felt able, he guided himself to the crescent of debris on which she stood. When his boot touched the edge of her platform, the shock of contact flipped his stomach and he doubled over. But the nausea passed and he straightened up. And he found himself face to face with Nerida, the sister who had survived so unexpectedly in this corner of darkness.

He wanted to touch her, to understand her material, to feel the hair that twisted from the crown of her head and floated towards him in slow waves.

'Hello,' Gavin said.

Nerida looked past him, her eyes on the ship. She gave no sign of having heard him.

Gavin used his hands to sign the official message: 'I come in humility to ask for your help.'

In one quick movement Nerida turned her back and crouched. A bony exoskeleton ridged her back. Images of hags in story books came to Gavin's mind. Gnarly old women squatting round cauldrons. He tried to banish these thoughts. Nerida had been out here for forty years, since that first failed mission. He did not understand what enabled her life, but he knew it was lazy to call it witchcraft.

Nerida stood, and beams of light spiralled from her hair and fractured into coloured grains. The grains brightened and glowed and spun. They were brighter than stars and suns, brighter than the light that bursts dark dreams. He told himself the spinning light was not sorcery but survival – exactly the kind of manipulation of material he was here to understand. He had seen images of this light before, in documentation of the doomed trips. Simon Miles had made him study the records from all previous missions. The rescue operation – launched too late to deserve the title. The research missions – at first undisguised attempts at salvage, then, when they discovered one of the sisters had survived, attempts to make amends, to reconcile, to understand.

One early explorer put his hands on the grains, so greedy for the information within them. The result: shattered neurons and wasted cells, his remains scattered across nothingness. Gavin was the latest in a line of explorers who had come to beg Nerida to tell them how she had managed to live out here. It did not feel real to have arrived, to be the one who stood before her, asking for help. But he did not reach out. He did not touch. He waited.

After a time, the light faded and Nerida pulled on a twist of hair. Specks of shining dust floated free as the strand detached from her scalp. She rose. She approached Gavin. He stood his ground. His heart raced. Her hand moved past his face, to the side of his helmet. Then her voice entered his ear, a fine dusting of whispered sounds. Her lips did not move as she said, 'What do you wish to know?'

He could not answer. He was mesmerised by her voice, its hush, its granulation. In his body, a jiggling of guts, liver, heart. His veins full of blood. His cock rising. They had joked, during training, about sex in space. Flaccidity. Fatigue. How it would always be novel athleticism rather than the satisfaction of desire. But his response, now, felt fragile and true.

What looked to be a smile flickered across Nerida's face. She looked at the ship. 'Who is with you?' she asked. A deep crease formed in her face, her shiny eyes sank deeper into her head.

Gavin was afraid. He knew what she was asking. He found his voice. 'Simon Miles is on the ship.'

Nerida made another sound. Too faint for a scream but with the same compressed emotion – anger, perhaps, or disbelief. Red shoots unfurled from her fingers like accelerated seedlings pushing through earth. Gavin was afraid. But he waited until the talons retracted. He could not imagine a soft body remained beneath her shell. The thought made him sad.

'You want to know what keeps me alive.' Her voice returned to a granulated hush. 'As the death of your world nears.'

'You're right. I want to know how you live, to see if we can also live. But only if you're ready to tell me.'

She pointed towards a sparkle in the distance. 'Phoebe,' she said. 'You must go to Phoebe.'

'Your sister? She… she also lives?'

'Yes. You must ask my sister to show you what we've learned.'

Nerida plucked a strand of her hair. And Gavin watched it change from twisting light to a dull, fine thread. She told him he must travel alone. The ship could not accompany him.

It was ridiculous, he thought. Dangerous. But it was more than anyone had been offered before. He let her wind the thread around his waist.

She pushed him from her platform, away from her beautiful exoskeleton, her loops of swaying hair, her grains of shining dust. Away too from his ship. Away from Simon Miles, an old man now, on his last mission, his last chance.

And as he drifted into space, guided by a strand of impossible hair, Nerida sang to him:

The fragile times
Of wasting minds
Can't shield your eyes
From fading stars.
Stay whole.
In muscle, vein, heart, brain.
Try not to fall.
But if you do,
Fall hard.

As Gavin floated across the vasty nothing, the deep darkness emptied his mind and he slept. It might have been a catnap. It might have been a fairytale thousand years. He did not know.

But he woke to see Phoebe.

She stood and shimmered at the entrance of a spinning rock of glitter.

Oh, Phoebe. A halo of glistening light at the mouth of an impossible construction. Her body was plump and cushiony; her posture relaxed, unsurprised.

As he neared her, a glittering speck brushed her cheek. She flinched and Gavin saw that, unlike Nerida, she had no exoskeleton. She raised her arm to stop another speck of light touching her face before turning back into her cave.

'Follow.' Her voice was high and clear. Gavin did not know what medium carried her words, but he knew he would obey any command she gave.

His weight returned as he stepped inside. He tried to ignore the nausea this time, telling himself it would pass quickly, trying to label the components of this new environment to distract himself from the discomfort. Wall. Floor. Air. Shimmer-coated walls, brightening as he stepped deeper. Stardust moulded as clay. He touched his hand to the wall to steady himself, and specks loosened and floated forward, into the cave's chamber, where Phoebe stood. She held her hands over her face. Red marks streaked her pale forearms. Gavin moved to her, to shield her, trying not to disturb any more light. She peered at him through her fingers. Another cut threaded across her face and he put his arms around her, his thick suit offering what protection it could until the cave became still.

Phoebe touched the strand of hair. It unwound from his waist and came apart in her hand. He didn't stop her as she reached up to take off his helmet.

'There now,' she said. 'I can see you.'

Her fingers were soft as she helped him remove his

suit. Minutes passed. Hours. Their touches slowed, stretched. An exploration.

'I'm the tiniest brightest star,' she said.

'You're beautiful, oh tiniest brightest star. I'm a giant meteor.'

'You look man-sized to me.'

'Perhaps I'm far away.'

'Don't say that.'

'Come here.' Gavin pulled her to him.

Sex was ecstasy, like he had heard it could be. Afterwards, they slept for a long time.

His heart woke him. Beats too rapid. Knocking questions against his ribs. Who am I? Why am I here? Am I a hero, a fool, nothing at all? He controlled his breath, centred his thoughts, as he had been trained to do. A happy place. A beach, sand, waves. Sunshine, brightness. A dog running. Sure of its own happiness. Everything was too bright. Phoebe asleep beside him. Soft pure light. He stroked her wrist. Warmth. Silver skin, as if it had been painted on. A pulse but no red veins beneath. No blood. New energy. Thrilling. She opened her eyes. Marbled stones with finely etched irises. Pale, pale blue. A blink of fair lashes. Tiny tubes. So strong. Her hand on his. Drawing his fingers between her legs. I am everything, he thought. I am nothing at all.

By the time they woke again, his questions had evaporated. Hours passed. Days. Before he asked again.

'But was your transformation gradual, or a sudden metamorphosis?'

'I'm trying to explain,' she said.

'I know. But you're talking in abstractions. If you could just give me the facts. Did you know what was happening to you at the time?'

'I'm trying to tell you.'

'We're going in circles.'

'Don't sigh. Please. I can string some facts together for you if you like.'

'Please.' His vocal chords were stretched and sore. Dry strings in his throat. 'I saw footage of you and your sisters in training. You looked so carefree. You turned cartwheels inside the simulator.'

Phoebe smiled. 'Yes. Those were good days. Exciting. So we trained, and we were… delighted in ourselves. We knew we would be selected for the mission – it wasn't arrogance, it was truth.' She smiled at him. 'We were selected. We went on the mission. We left the ship. The door would not open to readmit us. They left us here. These are the type of facts you want, yes?'

'It was terrible. I know. To be left behind. But then? What happened to you?'

'We had our suits. We had materials to construct a shelter. We had questions. And we had stories – stories about bodies destroyed and turning into other bodies. But most of all we had a will to survive. For all of us to survive together. You have that will too. I can see it. I know you understand.'

'And you did survive. You and Nerida survived.'

Phoebe hunched her shoulders, seeming to gather herself into as small a space as possible. 'We had to work quickly. We called up everything we knew. We were in a panic. We were angry. We were abandoned.' She looked up, her eyes searching. 'Have things changed back there? We thought we were part of the future. Of things becoming more equal between people. Between men and women, especially. We were dismayed that we were so dispensable, our gains so easily lost.'

'You were pioneers. Still are. What you have done—'

She interrupted: 'You have brothers and sisters?'

'I'm an only child.'

'You want to survive for your parents, your colleagues?'

'I want to survive so I can become who I am meant to become.'

'An explorer. A hero.'

'A son. A friend. A father, perhaps.'

'You have a woman for that?'

She was as old as his grandmother, he thought. 'Can you…?'

'New growth here is energy, not flesh and blood.'

'How did you start it? The change?'

'Now that's a term. The change.'

'I'm sorry.'

She shook her head. 'Time works differently out here.'

'The stories, about bodies. What were they?'

'You want facts.'

'Whatever you want to tell me. I'll listen.'

'They said in training that we had to control ourselves. But we refused to hold back. We were seen as mysterious, dangerous.'

'You aren't seen like that now,' Gavin said.

'We're ridiculous.'

'You're not ridiculous.'

'*We're* ridiculous. All of us. Trying to make sense of it.' She covered her face with her hands. Her shoulders heaved.

'I'm sorry it's difficult to talk about. I don't want to cause you pain. But you're our only hope.'

'That sounds familiar.'

'I need you.'

She shook her head. 'I can give you the facts. But I can't show you how to put them together. Collis will have to show you that.'

'Collis – your other sister?

'Our big sister. The lightest and brightest of us all.'

'She lives?'

'I do not know if any of us truly lives.'

'You feel alive to me.' Gavin saw the words flake from his lips. Their patterns in Phoebe's light. This is madness, he told himself. She is driving me mad. But her fingers on his face were like that first time.

'I don't know how anything works,' he said. 'How much time has passed?'

'We want time to stay soft.'

'We don't... that's not how things work.'

Sex was ecstasy. As they knew it could be.

Gavin woke from a dream of Phoebe turning cartwheels. Phoebe slept on in the centre of the cave, her light held tight within her. Gavin was restless. He walked to the mouth of the cave, knowing now to keep his hands away from the walls. Outside, the blackness stretched.

'Gavin?' Phoebe called. 'What are you doing?' Her voice was so full of music. 'Did you see anything good?' she asked when he came back in.

'Good? Like what? What is there to see?'

She shrugged. 'There's me. There's you.'

'It's not enough.' As the words left his mouth he realised their truth.

She closed her eyes as if she was in pain again.

'I have a mission,' Gavin said.

She turned on her side. Her back was rigid, reminding Gavin of her sister, Nerida.

'I have a mission,' he said again, gentler this time.

She turned. 'What's your mission, Gavin?'

'You know what it is. To find out… You know what it is.'

'To find out how we survive. To save yourself.'

She rose and went to the corner of the cave. She held up his helmet. A speck of light struck her forearm and a red dot appeared.

'Can't you stop it from hurting you?' he blurted.

Phoebe was radiant, her smile full of energy as she came to him. He tried to refuse the helmet but Phoebe stilled his hand, placed it over his head. There was a sharp whirring noise.

'Listen,' she said. 'I'm letting you hear it for yourself.'

'How could you send him out there?' Simon Miles's voice said inside the helmet.

The answer came in Nerida's dusty words: 'He wanted to go. Anyway, you didn't try to stop him.'

'But another death—'

Nerida interrupted: 'How do you know he's dead?'

'The others who came to you, they're dead.'

'Like me? Like my sisters?'

Gavin looked at Phoebe. She was listening, head bowed.

Simon Miles said, 'What do you want me to do?'

Nerida hissed. 'Nothing. You're good at that, aren't you?'

Simon Miles sighed. 'The ship must return. Soon. With or without Gavin. Please, just tell me if he's dead.'

There was silence for a few seconds.

Gavin touched Phoebe's arm. 'Am I… dead?'

Phoebe shook her head. 'But he won't be able to wait much longer. You must decide.'

'Decide?'

'You can go back to your ship. There is enough time.'

'How much time?'

'If you go back and tell them about me, then others will come.'

His heart beat hard and he wondered how many beats he had left.

Phoebe breathed in. The pores of her skin glowed. She looked brighter, harder. Ready for the others who would come.

'You could teach us so much,' he said.

'I've told you all I can.'

'But if you don't understand how you live, then how do you live?'

Phoebe laughed. 'Collis will like you. She was always one for the truth of things.'

'I don't know what to do.'

'You want more, Gavin. It's your nature. You can't help it. Collis is also this way. She'll tell you, I think – I hope – what you need to know. Let me help you get ready.'

At the mouth of the cave, she put her mouth to his, and he knew it was exactly the right amount of energy to send him to Collis. As he drifted away, Phoebe sang to him:

She condenses,
Into coldness,
Into ice.
As her tail swirls behind her
Her body ignites.
A perfect trajectory.
An arc of flame. Pure energy
That burns in minds,

In memories,
In visions
Of light.

Take sky
Take crystals
Weave them in.
Take dust
Take rocks
Take rays of sun.
Take sheets of lightning
Thunder clouds.
Gasp air.

Capture sound.
Take thoughts of love,
The thing itself.
Take nothing more
Then something else.
To make the loom
That weaves the stuff
From endless life,
Take just enough.

Time shifted again. Gavin refused to think about the risks. He asked himself questions. What would happen to children born in zero gravity? Would their bones develop? Would their limbs be withered and useless? Would their ears respond to different sounds? Would their brains overload with infinity as the vasty nothing shaped their personalities? Images of Phoebe hurdled his defences, gleeful as they filled his thoughts. Phoebe, a shelter from time, abstract and mutable, stretching his mind until it could no longer hold anything in place.

He felt Collis was near. His body felt her pure, condensed energy. The eldest sister. The lightest and brightest of them all. He searched for her but saw nothing. Her voice, though – her voice reached him like the legs of spiders spinning, stroking, conducting her words.

'What have my sisters done to you, oh little man?'

Gavin said his line: 'I come in humility to ask for your help.'

Crackling static, stabbing his ears, jangling his ribs.

He breathed and felt Phoebe's love, buoying him. 'I'm sorry for what happened to you out here. I'm sorry for what happened to you and your sisters.' It sounded like the truth.

'I am not sorry. I am all I was meant to be. I ask again, what have my sisters done to you?'

'Helped me. Saved me. Sent me to you.' Loved me, he said to himself as Phoebe's brightness warmed his skin.

'We were used by men like you. You claim humility, but you are full of arrogance. You want to formalise and control. You are prepared to sacrifice others to fuel your knowledge.'

'We cannot survive without your help.'

'Then you cannot survive. My sisters should have known better. They are as foolish as you.'

'Nerida is magnificent. And Phoebe—' his voice broke on the word. 'I have to complete my mission. Then I can go back to her.'

'You can't go back. You can never go back. Your desire is banal. We have moved beyond such bland oppression.'

A tear formed in the corner of his eye, stinging the soft cells there. It punctured his skin as it rolled down his cheek.

Collis's words ground on. 'Oh, Phoebe. She always took comfort in such things as love. She could not see you were a child. A vulnerable speck doing what your elders tell you. You will do what I tell you now. I will speak and you will listen.' Soft raspings – sobs or laughter. The sounds lengthened and filled his ears, emptying his mind of self. Dragging him to nothing.

'Please,' he whispered with his last reserves. 'Please. Will you tell Phoebe I did not want to leave her?'

As Gavin floated into space, Collis did not sing.

Phoebe put her fingers to her mouth, where his lips had brushed hers. She shut her eyes and saw Gavin's hopeful face. The brave explorer. Searching for knowledge to save his world. She had tried to tell him. He had talked about her past, her training, dredging up memories of life back there, the people who had left her out here to die. But she had not died. She had lived, and Gavin had found her. And now she hoped for him to live as she had never hoped before.

WHEN THE TIME IS RIGHT

F. B. Marbhán

Marguerite's hand stilled in mine. I didn't want to look up, didn't want to see the doctor's face. They were careful with their features. Smooth, unreadable. Warm eyes to disguise the truth, but I always knew. More bad news, more negatives and referrals and tests.

We wanted to do this together. Had wanted to. The first time, when we'd tested, Marguerite's hands had been slicked with sweat in my own. I could feel her heartbeat thrumming along her thumb, tensing as we had been told. The problem was me. Genetics, the district I'd grown up in, my line of work – they weren't sure. That was the first referral. Here, now, three years later, we still had no answers, and Marguerite's hand was dead in mine. There because she felt it should be, more than because she wanted it to be.

As the doctor began her list of things we could try, I could feel the fight we'd have later coming on. I wasn't ready to give up. We'd said we would do this together, and I had to hold on to that. Our dream. Even if Marguerite had lost hope. Even if, deep down, I had too.

Stepping into the lift, she let go of my hand and I prayed we wouldn't start fighting. Not yet. I could feel the excitement of those around us, the glowing faces, the pride of those who could, who would. Not us though, or at least, not me. The descent was slow, each ad that played over the glass surfaces causing my shoulders to wind tighter. Causing Marguerite to grow colder.

Until, 'For fuck's sake.' Bitterness twisting her face, her tongue. Coldness turned razor sharp, as though she could crack the glass around us. Shatter the truth.

Other people in the lift turned to look at her. I didn't need to look up to know what ad was playing; it was a miracle we'd made it this far down without it playing. The fight between us swirled, a storm about to break. A blizzard of Marguerite. The doors slid open, the flashing light of the 'G' above them giving me hope. We just needed to make it to the car. We could fight there, in privacy, without all those people knowing. Without their whispers and pity. Without their realisations and covered mouths, as if I was catching. I didn't need it. I just needed to get Marguerite to the car.

I pulled my mask up over my mouth as we stepped out onto the street and the lift doors slid closed behind us. Bad enough they'd know how poor we were, that we had to risk the city smog. At least, they wouldn't hear Marguerite. Wouldn't hear her vent my shame, wouldn't know the reason we couldn't afford the safety of underground parking.

I started walking. Marguerite seething behind me, the mask barely muffling her rage as we made for the car. Three years of appointments and specialists. Three years of waiting and hoping. Three years of saving everything we earned only to be told no. It was more than the money. I could feel the cost of it, in how we always seemed on the edge of a fight. Of how we lay side by side each night, both awake but neither reaching for the other.

In her fingers, cold and distant in mine whenever she felt it was needed, but not wanted.

Her car door closed seconds after mine, sealing us in. I didn't remove my mask as I started the engine, hoping she'd take the hint. Damp recycled paper rough against my lips, making it hard to get a complete breath, keeping the smog out. Keeping any molecules out, including any traces of oxygen still hanging around. I'd forgotten we couldn't afford ad free anymore. It began, playing across the windscreen as the engine idled. The same ad from the lift. The same ad that followed me around, haunting me. Taunting me.

'Marguerite,' I began, as her fists hit the dash.

'Don't. Don't fucking start, Elayne.' Her eyes swam over the edge of her mask, dripping onto her knees. Grit and sweat and smoke, like mascara in black and white. The smiling faces and bright lights of the ad turning them to miniature screens. More places for the ad to ruin me.

There was no escape. From the ads, from the fight. From her finally admitting our dream was over. From the future we would never have together, that played out in front of us, tantalising and torturing. As the last words flashed, 'your future, your past', I hit the accelerator. She'd need to get home, get her things; she wouldn't need much, but she'd probably take it all anyway. Take away every part of her, everything that had been Marguerite and Elayne and just leave me. The defective one. The one who couldn't be like everyone else. The one who'd ruined all our dreams of a family and a future together. The broken one, shattered against the bright lights and smiling faces of happy people, against every glass surface that flashed the words sent from the past to destroy me.

But Marguerite didn't deserve that. Her future, her past. That's what they told us, what the constant ads told us. I'd always taken it to mean 'your' plural, but now it would be singular. I, would be singular. The last wretched woman in this wretched future we'd made for ourselves. That they'd made for us. Just me and all the other poor saps who couldn't time travel dying in the smog of a past we would never see.

We had to sit through another ad before we could get out of the car. I watched Marguerite's face instead, still shining with her tears, and, for the first time in a long time, bright. From the ad, and with hope. Your future, your past. Hers.

She didn't look at me as she left, later.

The future was mine, and mine alone.

THE CONSTELLATIONIST

S. J. Menary

It began as a deafening scrape. The proximity siren wailed, strobes wildly dancing across the walls. The impact hurled me across the sterile floors.

'WARNING! WARNING!' announced UTA Drone Reaper Automated Spacecraft 0012475012. 'HULL BREACH. OXYGEN VENTING ON LEVEL TWO.'

I scrambled to my feet and reached for the virtu-screen console.

'DRAS, what's happening?'

'We have been in a collision,' the automated voice replied helpfully.

'I know that, DRAS! Damage report, execute now!'

'Executing.'

'You're an interstellar hydrogen gas reaper with a state-of-the-art long-range material scanner. And you still can't come up with anything less bleedingly obvious than "We have been in a collision,"' I muttered, raking over the scanner's screen. There was nothing out there but empty space.

I ran to the slit of Perspex that served as our only window in the corridor. A massive hunk of space junk was crushed up against the side of the ship. I squinted around the edges, but the window was so damn narrow. All I saw was a rusted-up mass of junk.

'Life support failing. Critical damage on level two and six. Oxygen venting complete on level two. Oxygen venting beginning on level one. Oxygen-hydrogen rupture safety mechanism engaged. Caution advised.'

'How did we not see that lump of ancient space debris?!'

'Life support terminated. ABANDON SHIP.'

'Oh crap!' I ran to the emergency room and grabbed the nearest spacesuit. Hauling the oxygen tanks onto my back, I heard DRAS's muffled announcement: 'Oxygen venting complete.'

DRAS listed suddenly to the starboard side, and I found myself sprawled on the floor and slammed against the airlock door. I felt a crack as my wrist hit the metal. I glanced down at the emergency control system attached to my wrist to see a giant crack running across the screen.

'Damn it!' I cursed as I realised that the impact had broken the heating element in my spacesuit. Without heating I'd freeze to death with the life support offline.

A crackle ran through the speaker in my helmet.

'…err, hello? Anyone reading me? Over.'

'What?' There was a little blinking yellow light on my wrist console under the broken casing. The communication link was still working! It was hardwired to pick up all rescue frequencies, and the light was blinking under the *Radio Wave Frequency* tab. I pushed down the receiver. 'Yes? Hello? Who is this?'

'Err, hello there… Madam? This is Herbert Bithersea, Captain of the *Magnum Opus*. I am terribly sorry, but I think our space ships have crashed. Are you hurt? Do you need assistance? Over.'

'Crashed?'

'I'm in the ship you just hit...'

'That lump of space crap?' Outside, I could just make out a little porthole in amongst the metal chunks attached with rivets. A person was standing by it, waving.

'Well, steady on there. "Space crap" is a bit strong...'

'And what do you mean "I hit you"?'

'Err... let me attach my docking cables and we can... um... exchange insurance details? Over.'

'Over what?'

'Nothing. Over.'

I sighed. 'Fine, but I hope you have an airlock on your "ship" because the oxygen and the heat are out on mine.'

I waited by the airlock doors until I felt the clunk of the cables attaching, doors interlocking and swooshing open. It was already warmer.

'How old is this rust bucket?' I wondered aloud.

The corresponding airlock door opened. As I stepped through, my eyes took a moment to adjust to the gloom. I was on a gangway lined with old wooden planks, surrounded by ladders and lockers and piles of stuff. There were empty paint cans stacked by the door, a pair of workmen's overalls strewn aside and what looked like an antique tin with a spout suspended from the ceiling. I ran my finger along the top of one of the lockers. Bright ferric dust came away on the shiny surface of my gloves.

At the end of the corridor, I saw a faint light. As I drew closer I saw him. He wore a blue velvet hat, too tall for the passageway, and had a large ginger moustache. He wore clothes that looked suited to another century – waistcoat and a gold chain looping from one of the pockets. But underneath, his face was young – about 25 I would have estimated, around the same age as me. He gave me a little wave.

'Err… hello. Welcome aboard the *Magnum Opus*. I'm Herbert. Do you speak Terrainian?'

'Yes, of course I do!' I snapped. 'We just spoke on the emergency broadcast channel, didn't we?' I pulled off my helmet.

And his mouth dropped open. Hurriedly, he took off his hat and put a hand out to shake mine. An antiquated custom and thoroughly unhygienic. I declined the offered appendage.

'Delighted to make your acquaintance. As I say, I'm Herbert Bithersea, but you can call me Bertie if you like. Everyone else does.'

I looked around. No one else was here. Well, almost no one. There seemed to be a creature huddled behind his feet. I recoiled in alarm. 'There is a pest aboard your vessel! Do you have a contamination issue on this ship?'

'What, Tesla? Oh no, he won't hurt you. Tame as a fly.' He touched the animal on the head and ruffled its floppy brown ears. 'Tesla's a good dog, aren't you boy?'

The emergency broadcast link beeped inside my helmet. DRAS's voice rippled upwards.

'Incoming call from Clone Superior 1214. Do you wish to respond?'

'Hold call,' I responded.

'Not advisable,' DRAS crooned.

'Hold,' I barked. 'I'll call her back.'

'Err…?' Herbert questioned.

I held up a finger. 'DRAS, begin auto-repair sequence diagnostic. Update me with the full damage report and then proceed to implement self-repair mode.'

'Affirmative,' DRAS replied.

'Miss?'

'What is it, Captain Bithersea?'

'Um, is it Miss? Can I call you Miss…?'

'You want my serial number?'

'Yes. It would help for the um… paperwork if I had your name?'

'Name? I am Clone 5476.'

'You're a clone?'

'Yes. Isn't that obvious?' I pointed at my face.

'Well… the last clone I met was a sheep… so no, not really.'

'Where have you been living? Under a moon rock? Of course, I'm a clone. I'm a model 54 – we are literally everywhere on Earth. And we all look exactly the same.' I recalled the face of my genetic ancestor. Jet black hair, and the melting brown eyes, what they once called Asian in race. A perfect copy of a perfect human female in every way.

'Oh. Oh, well that explains a lot. We don't get many clones out here on the fringes of the galaxy. I haven't been to Earth for a very long time.' He looked uncomfortably at his shoes. The animal behind him whimpered. 'I suppose that means you have a large family then?' he smiled at his own joke.

'No. Clones don't have families. Don't you know that? Clones aren't real humans. We don't have any of those human relationships. We are workers. Why would we need anything like that? But that is beside the point. What was your craft doing all the way out here, anyway? Don't you know there are international mining routes running through this part of space?'

'My crew and I pass through here quite regularly. I suppose you would call us a sort of floating clinic. We have a doctor aboard who does the rounds of the fringe planets. And I do the mechanical doctoring, you could say.'

'I don't understand.'

'Sorry. I'm a mechanical inventor. I do repairs mostly, a little tinkering with antiques and the odd commissioned piece. I helped to build this spacecraft.'

'You don't say.'

'It's mostly pre-Nano technology. Electrical components, even the odd bit of clockwork.'

'Clockwork? What is this, the 1800s?'

He pulled the gold chain from his pocket. At the end was a circular gold pendant. He thrust it towards me, its long chain still attached to his waistcoat with a pin. 'This is my favourite piece.' He flipped it open. The skeleton mechanism showed all the working cogs behind the decorative hands. 'This pocket watch tells the time in 48 different planetary time zones!'

'Why do you need one of these… pocket watch things? Don't you have a virtu-screen to tell you that?'

'It's not really the same, is it?'

'Seems like a waste of time to me.'

'Well, what do you do for a living then?'

'I'm a long-range space mineral reaper.'

'You're a hydrogen miner?' His eyes flashed for a moment, and he put his hat back on his head.

'Yes. UTA Drone Reaper Automated Spacecraft 0012475012 is my first command assignment. I've come to harvest the Caspar 1217 Nebula.'

'You're here to destroy the Bleeding Heart Nebula?'

'The what?'

'That's what we call it around here. You know, because of the legend?'

'No, I don't. And the sooner I can get back to my job the better.'

He turned away, his shoulders clenched. For a moment he said nothing. 'Your ship…' he said at last, turning back to face me. 'The UTA Drone Reaper Automated Spacecraft 001247… err… whatever. Is it damaged?'

'Nothing DRAS can't repair herself, I doubt.'

'DRAS?'

'It's just a familiar name. A little catchier than UTA Drone Reaper Automated Spacecraft 0012475012, don't you think?'

'Sure.'

'Anyway, she'll be good as new soon enough. These miner class vessels are notorious for venting life support at the smallest bump. It's the oxygen-hydrogen rupture safety mechanism. The designers were terrified that a hydrogen-oxygen leak would blow the ship into a million pieces.' I sighed. 'Look, my scanners didn't pick you up. It said the path was clear. And they were only recalibrated a few months ago. I set them to scan for carbon elastic molecules, tungsten and high-grade plastics. You know, the common ship building materials? What's this ship made of, anyway?'

'Iron.'

'Iron? Seriously? You're kidding?'

'Nope. Maggie may be a slow old bird, but she's nigh on indestructible. I'm surprised you didn't see us. Most people just go around…'

'So it's my fault, is it?'

'I didn't say that,' he patted one of the bulkheads. A cloud of rust emerged. 'I know it's not the usual building material, but Maggie has… character! And anyway, didn't you see us out of the windscreen? We are quite hard to miss!'

'Windscreen? Why would I need one of those? I've got a scanner.'

'And that worked out so well for you! All that technology and no windscreen!' He stifled a laugh.

I turned back to the airlock. 'Just message me the insurance details.'

'Wait! Wait, I'm sorry. I didn't mean to offend you, Miss. You can't go back on that ship; there's no life support.'

'Watch me,' I spat.

'But didn't you also say there was no heat on your ship? Will your spacesuit keep you alive?'

'Damn it. The heating controls got smashed in the accident.'

'Stay, and I'll make us a nice cuppa.'

The animal whined and looked up at me with hopeful eyes.

'Stay here? The whole place is unhygienic, and you have wildlife aboard.'

'But it is nice and warm…'

'Fine,' I hissed. 'I'll stay. But just until the life support is back up and running.'

'Grand,' the captain rubbed his hands together. 'I'll put the kettle on.'

The captain led me through a clutter of passageways, and I had to keep ducking to avoid hitting my head on dangling wires, coils of rope and what looked like the spokes from an ancient bi-wheeled self-driven transporter.

He ended the tour in a small chamber he called the kitchen. The walls were taken up with several pine lockers, and it had a huge wooden table crammed in with old-fashioned chairs wedged around it. The ceiling had been papered over, access panels and all, with yellowed strips featuring a repeating pattern of extinct mallards flying in formation.

'Please, make yourself at home,' the captain said, and proceeded to boil water in a primitive metal container. 'After we have had some tea, I'll get the insurance documents for you.'

I turned away and pressed a button in my helmet to return Clone Superior's call.

'Clone 5476!' she yelled as the call connected, her voice disturbingly similar to my own. 'You had better have a good explanation for ignoring my call! Our sensors show a collision. Report!'

'Affirmative!' I snapped to attention. 'At 1306 hours Terranian time a collision occurred between the UTA Drone Reaper Automated Spacecraft 0012475012 and a civilian craft upon arrival at the Caspar 1217 nebula. UTA Drone Reaper Automated Spacecraft 0012475012 sustained damage and the automatic hydrogen-oxygen rupture safety mechanism engaged, forcing evacuation from the vessel. Life support terminated. Sustained damage to heating controls on spacesuit during collision so emergency evacuation procedure was followed. Self-repair sequence initiated. Diagnostic report pending. End initial report.'

'Status?'

'Evacuated to colliding vessel.'

'You are on board a civilian craft?'

'Yes, Clone Superior. The *Magnum Opus*, Captain Herbert Bithersea, human, class unknown. It appears to be an archaic vessel built of a ferric compound. This would explain why the scanner did not detect it, Clone Superior.'

'Ferric?'

'Yes, Clone Superior.'

'And the human? Hostile?'

I eyed the captain pouring boiling water into a ceramic spouted vessel. He placed a striped hat on top and patted the bobble on the lid. 'No, Clone Superior. I don't think so.'

'You're not there to think, Clone 5476. You are there to accomplish. Report back on the diagnostic. And don't keep me waiting again.'

'Yes, Clone Superior.'

The captain brought his hatted-vessel to the table. He handed me a cup with a cartoon sun smiling on the side; a speech bubble drawn on its mouth read 'Sunny side up!'

'Please, Clone 5476… err, what do people call you for short?'

'For short?'

'Well, Clone 5476 is a bit of a mouthful,' he smiled. 'Please, sit down.'

I eyed the chair cautiously. No one, not ever, had expected me to sit in the presence of a full-blood human. And the captain was clearly no clone. But then, these were emergency circumstances and the arches of my feet were beginning to ache. I gingerly sat, peeking around the room to look for any hidden cameras that might be spying on my indiscretion.

'Apparently my birther called me Jara for convenience before I was weened, from what I have read in my personnel records. But no one has called me that since then.'

He placed a metal mesh over my mug and began to pour. Brown liquid tumbled in, leaving leafy fragments behind.

'Then, I shall call you Jara, if that's ok with you?'

I nodded absently. A tightening in my stomach was making my whole body start to shake. This… informality with a human. It felt wrong. So very wrong! I could feel the cold sweat begin to pool under my arms, my throat constricting.

'How do you take your tea?' he asked nonchalantly.

'Err…' My throat dried up. 'In a rationette,' I squeaked.

'You mean those awful plastic pouches you put in the microwave? Good grief! I wouldn't even give one of those to the dog! Would I now, Tesla?' The dog slumped on the floor by his feet and sighed.

'No, no, no. That simply won't do, my dear. This is the finest Darjeeling in interstellar space! Well…' – he stopped, and twirled the end of his moustache – 'it's about as close to Darjeeling as you can get this far north of the Milky Way, anyhow. It's actually a blend from Bakari 12. Remarkable climate for tea growing out there. My crew and I passed that way a few months back. They are all at the Taulel Bazaar at the moment. A few months shore leave to spend their money. I thought I'd take the opportunity to get out to the nebula and indulge my more spiritual interests. Milk and sugar?'

'Milk? Fresh milk?'

'Oh yes. We have a cow named Dolores on deck 4. She has a lovely temperament.'

'On deck 4?!' I could feel my head begin to spin.

He poured milk and stirred sugar into my cup, handing it to me personally. I baulked so hard I almost fell off my chair.

'Humans don't serve clones!' I exclaimed.

For a moment, the captain just looked at me as if I were an odd specimen he had come across. And then he shrugged.

'Suit yourself,' he said, popping the mug onto the table. He turned and began to rummage in one of the cupboards. 'Now, where did I put those Hobnobs.'

My mouth hung open in disbelief. What planet was this strange person from? How did he not know the rules that governed all our lives? *Human over clone, clone over drone, and that is how it is done.* I learnt this mantra before I could understand what a clone or a drone even was. But it is the natural order of the Empire. Full-blood humans come first, no matter what. And clones and drones serve them. This is the way of things. So why not here? Why not with him?

'Hobnob or custard cream?' he said to me, offering me a tin he had opened. 'It's a big decision. Take your time.'

'Hob… nob?' I wondered out loud, not really sure what he was asking me to decide between.

'Well, they aren't actually Hobnobs themselves. But about as close as you can get out here. I guessed the recipe and gave it to a chap out on Devra Prime who makes them up for me. We worked together a while back. Very decent chap. He makes them as a favour to me. They freeze brilliantly!'

Numbed, I took a crumbly orange food circlet and chewed. A warm comforting feeling filled me. I looked down at the circlet. It was so tactile, so messy, so…

different. I remembered the last time I had taken in nutrients. We had just reached the Caspar 1217 Nebula.

'Congratulations,' DRAS had announced. 'You are now the first official life form to reach Caspar 1217 and claim this mining territory for the United Terrainian Empire.' A little hatch had popped open under the console and out came the electronic distribution system. That thin, spindly metal arm had offered me a little plastic package. 'Please enjoy this sparkling wine flavoured liquid rationette, 0% alcohol, with the compliments of the Empire to congratulate you on your conquest.'

I'd drunk the saccharine gel as I'd started the preliminary calculations for the first stages of the mining operation. It had tasted like candyfloss – all sweetness on the outside and nothing of importance on the inside. A bit like me, I suppose. I'm a clone, remember. I'm not supposed to have the same things on the inside as true humans. No purpose, no spirit, no soul. Well, it's not like we have one, do we?

But this… Hobnob… it tasted like, well, what I imagine love must feel like. Someone had created this with their own hands and given it to the captain in an act of friendship. Not a plastic microwaveable pouch in sight. Was this how humans really lived?

I could feel his eyes watching me as I ate it. His eyes sparkled, burning to ask the question everyone always asks me. The crumbs of his custard cream tumbled into his moustache, and he brushed them off quickly.

'Go on,' I said at last.

'Go on what?' He sprayed food particles through the air.

'Ask me the question that everyone asks the first time they meet a clone.'

'Um… would you like another Hobnob?'

I put down the circlet. 'Don't you want to know what it's like to be a carbon copy of someone else? If I share my memories with other clones? If my thoughts are even my own? Am I exactly the same person as every other Model 54?'

'Are you?'

'No!'

'Well, there you are then,' he patted Tesla.

'What does that even mean?'

'Are you hungry? I am distinctly peckish. I need more than biscuits.' He turned and began rifling through the cupboards.

'DRAS,' I called through the communication link. 'Damage report update?'

'Compiling,' DRAS informed me. It's funny to think that her voice is probably based on one of my cloned ancestors. She's a drone, so beneath me. But we are practically 'family' in a strange sort of way. 'Damage report. 35% damage to level 2 and 6. Auto-repairs have been initiated, 25% complete.'

'Time to completion?'

'Approximately two hours.'

'Urgh! Two hours? DRAS, how long until life support is back online?'

'Approximately 120 minutes.'

'So!' Herbert slapped two unhygienic cardboard cartons on the table. 'Lucky Charms or Findus Crispy Pancakes?'

'Neither. Captain Bithersea, as much as I appreciate this… hospitality… I really must insist that we complete the insurance data exchange so that I can get on with repairing my ship.'

'Oh. Oh, of course. I'll find the paperwork,' he got up and left the kitchen.

On the far side of the chamber was a small round porthole. I stood up and walked over to look through it, running my fingers over the rivets. Outside, I could see DRAS all scrunched up. The lights were on and the little mechanobots were beavering away to straighten her out.

'DRAS, can you hear me?'

'Yes, Clone 5476. What can I do for you?'

'Nothing,' I sighed. 'I just wanted to hear your voice. It's funny. My best friend is a ship. But you're more than just a ship, aren't you DRAS?'

'I am an interstellar gas reaper, class—'

'I know that, DRAS! That's not what I meant. I meant you are more than just technology. Technology doesn't seem the right word for what you are. You are an exact copy. We are clones together in the silence of deep space. Kin... I suppose. It's strange. I am not supposed to have kin. None of my own anyway. I am supposed to just be a replaceable tool...'

'Your soliloquy is very pleasant, Clone 5476. And I like to think of you as my best friend as well. It's nice to be treated as more than just a drone.'

'Thanks DRAS.'

'Clone 5476?'

'Yes DRAS?'

'You have an incoming call.'

'Clone 5476! Report!' Clone Superior 1214's voice barked through the intercom.

'Thanks for the heads up, DRAS,' I muttered.

'What's that? Speak up! Report!'

'Nothing, Clone Superior. My apologies.'

'Apologies? I don't want your apologies, Clone 5476. What is the status of your situation?'

'Repairs underway, Clone Superior. Approximate time to completion and reinitialising of life support is two hours. Host vessel is preparing insurance data exchange to process for any claim.'

'Oh, there'll be a claim alright. Can't you speed the process up? Every moment we lose to these avoidable repairs is time in the Empire's budget line.'

'I would go back aboard and assist with repairs, Clone Superior, but I would freeze to death.'

'And?'

'Well… then I'd be dead?'

'Don't get fresh with me, Clone 5476. Remember, you are simply a tool on this vessel. And I can liquidate you at any moment I deem you are beyond all use.'

'Liquidate?' I gulped, clutching my hand involuntarily to my throat.

'Yes. Your clone body was injected with a Sparky 4000 safeguard at birth.'

'A what?'

'A single use electrical kill switch. Implanted on top of your heart. You make one false move, missy, and I'll detonate that bad boy remotely. Remember, Clone 5476, you are entirely disposable and your ship is capable of automatic piloting. We don't need you. It's only busy work, after all – so you feel included in the great plans of the United Terrainian Empire. This is a direct order, Clone 5476. Return to your vessel and complete the repairs. End Call.'

I slumped against the wall and slid down it until I was sitting on a small table. I ran my hand over the skin on my chest. Sure enough, there was a little bump just above my heart. I'd always just assumed it was nothing. Now I knew. It was my death sentence.

'OK!' the captain announced, bursting into the kitchen. 'I've got the paperwork here. All we need to do is exchange details and sign here, here and—' He suddenly broke off from pointing out places to sign and looked up at me directly. 'Jara? Are you quite alright?' he asked with concern.

'My boss wants to kill me,' I moaned.

He knelt before me. 'It can't be that bad?'

'She implanted an electrical kill switch in my chest at birth.'

'Oh. That's... specific.'

'And she wants me to freeze to death back on DRAS to finish the repairs faster.'

'Ah. Well, we can't have that, can we?'

I dropped my face into my hands and began to cry. The sensation was so alien to me. 'What's happening?' I wailed. 'Clones aren't supposed to have feelings! We're supposed to be perfect and completely without any of these... messy... human... emotions!'

'Well, you are a clone of a human,' he said, placing a consoling hand on my shoulder. 'I'd say that makes you human enough.'

'That's not how it is! I was told from birth that I am just a copy. Human over clone, clone over drone, and that's how it's done. This isn't how it's done. This isn't perfect! It's all gone wrong! And why is there mucus coming out of my nose?' I snorted.

He pulled a square of material from his waistcoat pocket and presented it to me. 'Humans are flawed, messy, volatile creatures. We are imperfect by our very nature and we are made exactly that way from the beginning. Any human who tried to make us "perfect" in the past was, in my humble opinion, a psychopath. And human you must be. We are all made up of DNA, are we not?'

'I've never heard anyone phrase it like that before,' I sniffed.

'Well, it's what I believe. I suppose you might call it my religion. We are what we are – exactly the way we are meant to be. Just like the universe around us. No one tells the stars to be more perfect than they are, do they? Or the nebulas. They just are, and that's just fine. It's the reason I'm out here in the first place.'

'You're not one of those Constellationists, are you? Some crazy eco-warrior that wants to "save the universe" from the big bad Empire?'

'You might say something like that…' he said.

'What? You're one of those religious nuts that believes all nebula have souls or some other nonsense.'

I sensed him bristle at that.

'Well, you are actually sitting on my prayer altar…'

'Oh!' I leapt up and realised the little table I was perching on was spread with a blue cloth and littered with little candles and what looked like a model of a star made by a child. No wonder it was uncomfortable.

'Who puts an altar in the kitchen?' I wiped my nose on my sleeve.

'Some crazy religious nut?' he smiled. 'Come on, I'll show you.'

Herbert led me out of the kitchen and down a gangplank to a sealed doorway.

'This is the reason I'm here,' he said, pulling the door open.

As I stepped inside, the empty room flooded with gold.

'I remember...' I said slowly, grasping at the edge of a memory. 'I remember something like this. From when I was very young. I was in a room with my birther, I think, and there was sunlight flooding in...'

'Look up,' was all he said.

Above us, great arches of glass rose into space like the heart of an archaic cathedral. The nebula embraced us, winding around the ship and wrapping us in a blanket of stars.

'The colours...' I gasped. I reached out to touch the pink columns of gas, brushed through with vibrant purples and swirls of light.

Herbert flicked a switch on the wall and suddenly we were floating, the gravity drive suspended. Tesla gave a soft whine as his ears lifted and his legs batted.

Herbert took my hand, and we drifted up towards the roof. It was so close I could almost taste the tangerine clouds. My heart pounded, as if it had always yearned to see this and I only now understood.

'It's... it's so beautiful!'

'Have you never seen a nebula before?'

'Only as a 3D image. But this? It's like we are in...'

'Heaven?'

I looked across at him. His face was alive, eyes twinkling.

'Clones don't have heaven... but if we did...' I couldn't help smiling.

Herbert lay back, staring upwards. 'Legend has it that this nebula was once a great god. His name was Ammarnatu. He fell in love with a girl from Hallem-Lau. You can make out the curvature of the blue planet just

THE CONSTELLATIONIST

beyond that pillar of blue cloud. Can you see it? Well, her father disapproved of the match, and spirited her away to marry another. And Ammarnatu, destroyed by a grief, dissolved into this nebula until just his bleeding heart remained, forever.'

'His heart?' I asked.

'Turn this way. Do you see it? The reddish formation in the edge of the blue clouds over there?'

The heart of a long dead god, still bleeding an indigo streak of heartbreak. Just beyond, I could make out the darkness of space encroaching. 'It makes you feel... sad, thinking about it,' I said slowly.

'Exactly! That's what the locals say. This nebula – it has an aura about it. Something tragic that lingers. It used to be called ancestral memory, once upon a long time ago.'

'Is it true?'

'Who knows? I like to think so.'

'And the Empire wants to destroy it. And me, along with it. We will both be dead in space...'

Herbert swirled around to meet me. 'You don't have to do it. You could stay here. Be part of my crew. I don't care that you're a clone. You could have a life here, Jara. If you wanted it?'

'But if I don't carry on with my mission, I'll be liquidated anyway.' I floated down to the floor and pressed the gravity drive back on.

Herbert landed with a thunk. Tesla dropped on top of him with a little yelp.

'I'm dead if I do, and dead if I don't.'

'I can't force you to abandon your mission,' Herbert said, getting up and dusting himself and the dog off. 'I wish you would, but I can't ask you to risk your life either.

But you can be so much more than just a tool, Jara. You can be a person first, and make your own decisions.'

'All I know is that I don't want to die.'

'Maybe I have some equipment that might help you to stay warm aboard? At least that way you have a little more time to make your mind up?'

'You would do that for me? Even though I'm about to destroy your god?'

'Well, that's a simplistic way of putting it, but yes.' He took me by the shoulders and looked me straight in the eye. 'I know we haven't known each other very long, but I would rather like to think we might be forming a friendship here and I'd hate to have you freeze to death in the middle of it.'

'I've never had a real live friend before,' I smiled. 'Only DRAS.'

'Well, let's get you back on board with DRAS sooner rather than later,' he grinned back.

We tramped down another passageway, the wooden planks clattering under our feet.

'It's in here,' said Herbert, pulling open a locker door. A sea of electrical parts, wires and tools flowed out. 'Ah, don't mind the mess. Everything just gets thrown into the cupboard under the stairs.'

'What are we looking for?' I asked.

'I think I have some heating coils in here somewhere. If I add in a bit of insulation to stop it burning you to a crisp, I think it might do the job.' He threw electrical innards out of the junk heap. 'I'll need to tinker with it a bit, though. Oh, and we can use this as well!' He threw out another piece. He sat on the floor, screwdriver between his teeth, and set to work.

'Height feeze.'

'What?'

He spat the screwdriver out. 'Light please, and can you pass me a roll of electrical tape? I like the blue one.'

I passed him the roll from a box on the side, and switched on one of the overhead lights. 'You think it will work?' I looked nervously at the countdown of the repair time DRAS had helpfully sent over to my communication link screen.

'Should do. How much time do we have left?'

'40 minutes.'

He flipped open his pocket watch and nodded.

'EMERGENCY CALL!' DRAS yelled over the communication link.

I jumped. 'Go ahead.'

'Clone 5476! You were given a direct order! Your tracker says you are still aboard that host vessel. Why aren't you back on UTA Drone Reaper Automated Spacecraft 0012475012? You are supposed to be assisting with repairs.'

'Clone Superior! Forgive me. The captain of the host vessel has been assisting me to incorporate a warming element to my spacesuit so that I can return to the ship before life support is back online. He wanted to… help protect the Empire's assets?'

'The Empire's assets are none of his concern. They are ours to dispose of as we wish. Clone 5476, this is turning into a drain on our budgets. I'm afraid you have outlived your usefulness. I am going to have to liquidate.'

'What! No, please, I don't want to die!'

'I'll have to request authorisation from my superior. Stand by for further instructions.'

'No!'

'What is it?' Herbert leapt to his feet.

'They're about to liquidate me! Oh no, no, no!'

'Sit down!' he cried. 'How many volts are we talking about?' he demanded, tearing electrical tape off the roll.

'4000 I think? I think she said... I don't know!'

'Lean back,' Herbert pushed my shoulder back against the iron bulkhead. He pulled out his pocket watch. 'Where is the implant?'

I pulled my shirt open. 'Here – see, just under the skin.'

He fervently began to tape his watch to the wall. He unpinned the chain from his waistcoat and blew on the sharp point.

'What are you doing?!'

'I'm earthing you.'

'What?!'

'Incoming call,' DRAS announced.

'Clone 5476?' Clone Superior's voice chirped out of the communication link. 'We have approval. Liquidation sequence initiated. Prepare for immediate liquidation. Please note there may be a five second delay due to interstellar Wi-Fi buffering. End call.'

I scrunched my eyes up tight and tensed up for the shock. Herbert leapt to his feet.

'Sorry Jara. This is going to hurt,' he said, and he stabbed the watch pin into my skin. The piercing pain broke through my skin. The electricity hit me like a sharp, burning spark taking over my senses. Everything went black.

'Clone 5476? Please respond? Clone 5476? DRAS calling Clone 5476. Please respond.'

'Jara? Jara? Can you hear us?'

My whole body felt sore, but not the kind of sore you get with a bruise. No, this was a tingly sort of sore that still felt charged.

'Urgh.'

'Is that you Clone 5476?'

'Yes, DRAS. It's me.' I rolled over on the gangway. My ears were ringing. Loudly.

'Jara?' I could feel Herbert pulling me up from the floor. 'Are you alright? You've gone a funny shade of grey.'

I forced my eyes open and tried to make my legs stop shaking.

'That was a big old shock you got there.'

I looked up at him. He looked a little pale himself, and his magnificent moustache had frizzed out until it resembled an angry hedgehog. I reached for the burn on my own chest, wincing. There was a thin trickle of blood running across my fingers.

'I'll get you a bandage for that.'

'That was a bloody stupid thing you did,' I croaked. 'The current could have killed you as well. Why would you risk your life for me? I'm just a clone.'

'You're not just a clone,' Herbert smiled. 'And I couldn't just let them fry you. You're my friend, Jara.' He slapped me on the back, and I winced again. 'Maggie will have absorbed the current by now. She's plenty big enough to disperse the electricity. It should be safe by now. It's a good job that gold is such a good conductor too.'

'Your pocket watch? That was some quick thinking.'

Herbert pried the melted remains of his watch gingerly from the bulkhead with the edge of his boot. 'Alas, I

239

think she will not be telling the time in 48 planetary time zones anymore.'

'I'm really sorry about that.'

'Not to worry, Jara. It's just a thing. Things can be replaced. I think, all things considered, we deserve a cup of tea after all that.'

'Repairs complete,' DRAS exclaimed cheerfully over the communication link. 'Life support back online. Auto harvesting has been initiated by Clone Superior 1214.'

I looked at Herbert.

'The tea will have to wait. We have to stop the auto harvesting.'

'Are you sure?' he asked.

'Yes. They've already killed me. What else can they do to me?'

'I am sure they can think of a hundred horrible things to do to you.'

I looked down at the melted lump that was once Herbert's favourite pocket watch and touched the wound over my heart.

'But you were right, Bertie. I'm not just a clone anymore. I'm my own person, and I can make my own decisions about my future. I don't want to be just another tool for the Empire. They were going to liquidate me just because I was expendable! And you... you barely know me. But you saved my life. I'm going back aboard DRAS and I'm going to stop them mining the nebula. I have to show them that they can't just destroy whatever they think belongs to them.'

'Jara, I'll do whatever you need me to. Just say the word.'

'I need you to be ready to get your ship as far away as she can go.'

'That won't be very far.'

'Just be ready,' I said as I marched towards the airlock.

'Clone 5476. Your security clearance has been revoked on account of your death. Intruder Alert activated. Sorry,' DRAS said apologetically as I stepped aboard.

'I'm not dead yet, DRAS.'

I moved towards the console.

'I must advise you to leave, Clone 5476. I would not want you to get into trouble. You have five seconds until the sirens come online.'

'Do what you have to, DRAS.'

'WARNING, WARNING. INTRUDER ALERT!'

As I reached for the controls, a holographic image appeared in front of me. She looked exactly like me, but with Senior pips on her white uniform.

'Clone Superior!'

'Well, well, well, it looks like the Sparky 4000 needs to be upgraded. Clone 5476, you're still alive it seems.'

'Yes I am. And I'm putting a stop to this once and for all. I'm not your tool anymore, Clone Superior. This nebula is not Empire property and I am revoking your security clearance in this area!'

'You? Revoke my security clearance? Don't be absurd. Now step away from the controls like a good clone. We'll sort out the liquidation issue when you return, and until then you will confine yourself to quarters for the duration of this mission.'

'I will not.'

'Then I'll vent the life support and freeze you to death.'

'You do that.'

'OXYGEN VENTING. LIFE SUPPORT FAIL-
ING. TEMPERATURE DROPPING,' DRAS wailed.

I pushed through the hologram and grasped the
controls.

'What are you doing?' Clone Superior demanded.

With shivering hands, I typed in the sequence to stop
the auto harvesting.

'I'm ending this. The hydrogen in this nebula is not
yours to take. And I'm no longer your tool!'

'Clone 5476, cease and desist!'

'No!'

'Stop. This is futile. The control system for harvesting
has just locked you out. What do you have to say to that
then, Clone 5476?'

'Damn it!' Red blocking messages flashed up on the
screen. I dropped under the console. I could feel the cold
seizing up my joints. I pulled open the panel and began
pulling out the wires.

'That won't work, Clone 5476.'

'Come on!' I said to myself as I braced my foot against
the console and pulled at anything that I could tear out
with my hands. 'You have to stop this!'

'Stop the Empire's work? Hah!' Clone Superior
laughed. 'You have lost your mind, Clone 5476. Nothing
can stop the mighty will of the human United Terrainian
Empire. Human before clone, clone over drone, and that
is how it is done. Don't think for one second that this
puny display of rebellion will change anything.'

I got to my feet and faced the hologram. 'You think
that you are so much better than me? You're a clone too!'

'But I know my place, unlike you. That's why I'll be
alive in the next ten minutes and you'll be dead.'

The inside of my helmet was frosting over with ice flakes. My breath was coming out in foggy gasps. I looked down at my arms and they were iced with hoarfrost.

'So much for wanting to live,' Clone Superior smirked.

'But at least it's my life now. I get to choose how it ends.' I grabbed the fire extinguisher by the console and began to hammer down on the screens. The plastic shattered and splintered.

'Clone 5476,' DRAS said inside my helmet.

'I'm sorry, DRAS. I'm so sorry. It's not your fault... but... they have to stop!'

'I direct your attention to the lateral access panel.'

I looked across to where a panel had flipped open beside me. A large red button sat inside, yellow lights pulsing around it. I peered closer.

'DANGER: MANUAL OXYGEN-HYDROGEN RELEASE VALVE.'

'Wait!' cried Clone Superior. 'Don't touch that button, Clone 5476!'

'My name is not Clone 5476. It's Jara.'

'I'll rescind the liquidation!'

'What? You'd allow me to live?'

'Yes! And if you refrain from touching that button, I'll get my superiors to grant you... um... full-blood human rights back on Earth. What do you say to that? Just do your job and come home and you'll be free to do as you wish!'

'Jara, my scanners indicate that Clone Superior is lying to you,' DRAS informed me.

'Thanks, DRAS. I think so too.'

'I order you to step away from that button!' Clone Superior screeched.

'Please press the button, Jara,' DRAS insisted.

'But DRAS, if I press that button you'll explode. Isn't there another way?'

'There is no other way, Jara.'

'There has to be…' My teeth chattered together as a shiver shook my whole body.

'You never made me feel like a drone,' DRAS said inside my helmet. 'I appreciate that. Human with clone, clone with drone, and that's how it should be done. It has been a pleasure serving with you. Good luck.'

'Goodbye DRAS. It's been a pleasure serving with you too. I'll never forget you.'

I leaned over and pressed the button.

'WARNING, WARNING! HYDROGEN TANK CONTAINMENT BREACH. HYDROGEN VENTING INTO OXYGENATED ENVIRONMENT. COMBUSTION IMMINENT! EVACUATE! EVACUATE! EVACUATE!'

'What have you done?! Clone 5476! Clone 5476!' Clone Superior screamed.

I pounded towards the air lock and prised it open.

'40 SECONDS TO IMPLOSION!' DRAS cried gleefully.

'Bertie!' I shouted into the radio link. 'Open the door!'

The airlock scraped open, and I hurled myself inside as we broke free from the docking cables. Staring out of the porthole in the door, I watched as we moved away from DRAS, the sirens still ringing in my ears.

'Oh DRAS, I'm sorry,' I whispered.

The explosion hit us like a tsunami. All I saw was a flash of orange and then the *Magnum Opus* rocked like a leaf in a hurricane. I hit the wall with a force that drove all the air from my lungs, cracking the screen of my helmet.

I stood at the porthole staring out into the Bleeding Heart Nebula, pressing down on my communication link. Static frizzled back at me. I pressed again. Nothing. A tear rolled down my cheek as the light of the fires flickered against the glass.

'Jara!' yelled Herbert as he crashed down the passageway after the *Magnum Opus* stabilised. 'Jara, are you ok?' Tesla came loping along behind him.

'She's gone, Bertie. DRAS's gone. She did it to save me.'

I felt his hand softly on my shoulder. Tesla leant up against my legs, looking up at me with big sad eyes.

Where DRAS had been, a bright white light burst forth, swirling amongst the debris. Parts of her were splayed out in space, her hydrogen cargo imploding in stunning starbursts. Orange flares shot up as the oxygen burned away, to be replaced by tumbling fragments.

'Human with clone, clone with drone, and that's how it's done,' I repeated slowly.

'That has a nice ring to it,' Herbert said.

'DRAS was the only friend I ever had. And now she's destroyed.'

'No. DRAS isn't gone. She's there, look. This is the first stages of a new nebula being born,' Herbert said softly. 'It's incredible!'

I placed my hand on the cold glass, reaching out to touch DRAS one last time. The hydrogen gasses were coiling around, pure brilliant light forming into something that had not quite yet coalesced.

'This might be the closest thing to the divine that we will ever get to in our lifetime. Amazing!' he breathed. 'A brand new nebula, that will live on for millennia. Thanks to you.'

I put my hand on the glass.

'You did a good thing, Jara. DRAS would have wanted you to carry on.'

'I guess I have a life of my own now. Although I'm not sure what to do with it?'

'There's no rush to decide, and there'll always be a place for you on the crew here if you want it – I think you'd like it here.'

'I think—'

'First things first,' he interrupted me. 'Let's put the kettle on.'

AUTHOR BIOGRAPHIES

These are printed in alphabetical order by contributor surname

Max Bantleman

Max Bantleman is the editor of this volume. He is also a games designer, drummer, bass player, gamer and self-styled 'Great Old One'. He has written and edited science fiction for many years, as well as putting his talents towards writing/editing role-playing games, screenplays and military history. He has co-founded various writers' groups over the years and currently chairs the Banbury Writers' Café that meets every fortnight in Banbury, Oxon. He published his first novel, *SoulDice*, in 2017.

Melaina Barnes

Melaina Barnes is a writer and artist who grew up in the north of England and has lived in Cardiff, London and Lisbon. She has recently finished writing her first novel, and her short fiction has been published in *The Londonist* and *Litro Magazine*. Her stories are regularly performed at spoken word events, and her story 'Mud Man' won the British Academy's Literature Week competition.

Colette Bennett

Colette Bennett comes from a news background and for the past 11 years has written on everything from breaking news to

Asian pop culture. Her work has been published on CNN, HLN, The Daily Dot, Engadget and Colourlovers. She has also had features published in print in *Continue Magazine* and the Norwegian magazine *Aftenpolten Innsikt*. She is currently finishing work on her first novel, *Chasing the Ema*, a YA sci-fi tale about a young girl's journey to find the father she's never met.

Philip Berry

Philip Berry is a London-based doctor with parallel interests in medical ethics and creative fiction. (The fictional disease described in his story 'Bronzene' is inspired by a real condition called haemochromatosis.) He has published works of non-fiction, a series of books for children and two medical thriller novels – *Proximity* and *Extremis*. His sci-fi short stories have appeared in numerous anthologies and are now available in his own collection *Bonewhite Light* published in 2017.

Richard T. Burke

Richard T. Burke works by day as a systems and software manager for a hi-tech start-up company, and writes genre fiction by night. He is the author of three novels, *The Rage*, *Decimation: The Girl Who Survived* and *The Colour of the Soul*, as well as the short story 'A Christmas Killing' included in Bloodhound Books' charity horror anthology *Dark Minds*. He lives with his wife and daughter in the village of Rotherwick in Hampshire.

Philip Charter

Philip Charter is a writer and English teacher who lives and works in Pamplona, Spain. He is tall, enjoys travel and runs the imaginatively named website 'Tall Travels'. His fiction has been published in *STORGY*, *Fabula*, *Argentea*, *Carillon* and *The Fiction Pool* magazines among others. His piece 'Raft' won the 2018 WOW Festival flash fiction competition.

Sue Eaton

Sue Eaton became fascinated with science fiction from an early age, through her love of authors like Ray Bradbury, John Wyndham and Terry Nation. She is also a lifelong Whovian, who once managed to convince a trainer on a time management course that she had successfully fitted twenty-five hours into one twenty-four hour day. She has had her work broadcast on Radio 4 and her debut novel, *The Woman Who Was Not His Wife*, was published in 2018.

Kelly Griffiths

Kelly Griffiths lives with her husband and children in Northeast Ohio, USA. She describes herself as a creative, convoluted confessionist; and her stories have been published in *Reflex Fiction*, *The Drabble*, *Fiction on the Web*, *Zeroflash*, *Ellipsis Zine* and most recently *The Forge Literary Magazine*. She is currently finishing work on her first novel, *Trespass*.

Cathy Hemsley

Cathy Hemsley works as a senior software engineer for GE Power, but has been writing fiction in her free time for over ten years now. Her work has been published in *People's Friend*, and she has established a small writers' group in her home town, the Rugby Association of Fictioneers. In addition to writing short stories, she is currently working on three full-length novels. She is married with two daughters and also finds time to do voluntary work for a local charity for homeless people.

F. B. Marbhán

F. B. Marbhán is the pen name for Aoiffe Kenny, currently working on her Masters in Irish Folklore and Ethnology at University College Dublin. She writes short science fiction pieces, and fantasy based on Irish folklore and mythology. Her story 'Practical Time Travel' was recently selected for inclusion in the literary and art journal *HCE Review*. She has recently completed her first fantasy novel.

Nick Marsh

Nick Marsh has been writing for over twenty years and, although he still has plenty of time for his first love of writing short stories, he has branched out into plays and the occasional bit of poetry. One of his plays, *A Frank Exchange*, which tells the story of the person who betrayed the Frank family to the Nazis in Amsterdam 1944, won the National Drama Festivals Association's George Taylor Award for the best new one-act-play script in 2017.

Tegon Maus

Married 48 years to a woman he calls Dearheart, Tegon Maus lives a contented life in a small town of 8,200 in Southern California. By day, Tegon is a successful home remodelling contractor, but his passion is storytelling. He writes quirky sci-fi, contemporary fiction, action/adventure and other genres, all with a dash of humour. He is the author of seven books, including *Machines of the Little People*, *The Gift* and his bestselling title, *BOB*.

S. J. Menary

S. J. Menary studied archaeology and ancient history at the University of Birmingham, and now works as a museum development officer in Oxford. She writes horror, fantasy and steampunk stories, which have been published internationally in various collections. She has also written award-winning poetry. In her spare time, she is an active member of the Sealed Knot historical re-enactment society. She lives in Rugby, Warwickshire with her partner and two cats.

Morgan Parks

Morgan Parks lives in darkest Surrey with a senile cat, an optimistic Labrador and a variety of human family members. Between taming the garden, feeding the animals and drinking coffee, she reads a lot and writes a little. Her writing mostly emerges as sci-fi or fantasy and has been shortlisted for the James White Award and appeared in *The Casket of Fictional Delights*, *FlashFlood* and *Horror Scribes* – with her piece 'Two Hearts' winning *Horror Scribes'* Valentine's Day Competition.

Devon Rosenblatt

Devon Rosenblatt studied Media Production at the University of Lincoln and now works in the A/V team of the Oxford NHS Trust and as a freelance video and A/V editor. He has a passion for all aspects of media and has worked behind the scenes on the independent sci-fi film *Kaleidoscope Man* (2018) and received actor credits for the short *Damned Nation* (2018), the independent horror film *Bite* (2018) and the TV mini-series *The 7th Day*. Writing science fiction is another of his passions, and his story 'The Afternoon Affair' can be found in the anthology *Tasty Morsels*.

MM Schreier

MM Schreier is a New England native who writes a wide range of genres from creative non-fiction to contemporary, literary and speculative fiction. When not writing, MM Schreier can be found tutoring science and maths to students for whom English is a second language or hiking in the Green Mountains. Recent publications can be found in *Open: Journal of Arts & Letters*, *Ponder Review*, *Words & Brushes* and the Writer's Workout anthology, *Tales from the Cliff*.

Aviva Treger

Aviva Treger was born in Hastings, East Sussex. She studied Ancient History at University College London, then later trained as an actor with Questors Theatre in Ealing. She's a new writer, but her short stories have already been published in a number of collections including *England's Future History: Volume 1*, *Tales from the Forest*, *Idle Ink* and *Un-Turn This Stone* – the latter taking its title from her story 'Unturn This Stone' included in it.

Lewis Williams

Lewis Williams founded Corona Books UK in 2015. His literary endeavours have been multifarious, including most recently editing *The Second Corona Book of Horror Stories*. He has two degrees in philosophy (which number might be considered two too many) and worked for a number of years in a number of different roles for Oxford University before his ignominious departure from its employ.

Author Websites and Twitter Accounts

Those authors who have Twitter accounts and/or their own websites are listed below.

Max Bantleman	@MaxBantleman
Colette Bennett	@colettebennett
Philip Berry	@philaberry philberrycreative.wordpress.com
Richard T. Burke	@RTBurkeauthor rjne.uk
Philip Charter	@dogbomb3 talltravelling.blogspot.com
Sue Eaton	@SueJayEaton susanjeaton.com
Kelly Griffiths	@GriffithsKL Kellygriffiths.wordpress.com
Cathy Hemsley	isnarniaallthereis.wordpress.com
F. B. Marbhán	@clockworkselkie patreon.com/FBMarbhan
Tegon Maus	@TegonMaus Tirpub.com/tmaus
S. J. Menary	@sjmenary_author sjmenary.wordpress.com

Morgan Parks	@morganjparks
	morganparkswriter.wordpress.com
Devon Rosenblatt	@SpectralWeaver
	kuriousplanet.com
MM Schreier	@NoD1v1ng
	mmschreier.com
Aviva Treger	@Aviva321
Lewis Williams	lewiswilliams.com

Innovative, brilliant and quirky

Corona Books UK is an independent publishing company, newly established in 2015. We aim to publish the brilliant, innovative and quirky, regardless of genre. That said, we do have a fondness for sci-fi and horror!

For the latest on other titles published by us and forthcoming attractions, please visit our website and follow us on Twitter

www.coronabooks.com

@CoronaBooksUK

Readers who enjoyed the stories in this book by Sue Eaton and S. J. Menary may be interested in discovering *The Corona Book of Horror Stories*, which includes stories from both these authors. Sue Eaton's debut novel, the sci-fi thriller *The Woman Who Was Not His Wife*, is also published by Corona Books UK.